When Chris told his friend that he didn't want a mate, he didn't expect to meet his mate anytime soon. But here he is, a human mate to a Vila, and he's not sure what to do about it. He might not have wanted a mate, but he has one now, and being Gary's only chance at bonded happiness is a heavy weight.

Gary only ever wanted to be safe. After losing his clan and being on the run for years, he's found a place to call home, but nightmares plague him. When he meets Chris, he's delighted to have found his mate, but Chris is human and a hunter. Gary has already lost everyone he loves — can he bear to be with Chris when Chris has no plans to stop hunting Kudlaks?

Will Chris have to choose between what he feels is his duty and his mate? Or can Gary accept the way his mate willingly puts himself in danger?

This book is a work of fiction. Names, characters, places, and incidents either are products of the author's imagination or are used fictitiously. Any resemblance to actual events or locales or persons, living or dead, is entirely coincidental.

Garretson
Copyright © 2024 Catherine Lievens
ISBN: 978-1-4874-4169-2
Cover art by Angela Waters

Published by eXtasy Books Inc

Look for us online at:
www.eXtasybooks.com

GARRETSON
KRSNIK CLAN 3

BY

CATHERINE LIEVENS

Chapter One

The air smelled of dust and fresh wood. It had become familiar in a way few things were in Chris's life. Chris couldn't say he minded. In fact, he didn't. The smell reminded him that he was building his future.

He took a step back and stared at the wall in front of him. Okay, maybe his future would be a little crooked, but it was the thought that counted, right? The house didn't have to be perfect. It just had to be perfect for Chris, and as far as he was concerned, it was.

All the houses in the village needed work, including this one. It was decent enough that he could live in it, but every room needed a fresh coat of paint, and some needed more. He'd started getting rid of the old wallpaper, and the thought of the insects he was finding under it made his skin crawl. That was why he'd decided that painting would be easier than putting up new wallpaper, but he'd been wrong there, too.

It didn't matter. He was the only one living in this house, so he'd be the only one to see how crooked everything was. He had no idea what he was doing when it came to renovating his house, and he thought he was doing a pretty good job.

As long as he stayed away from anything more significant than painting, he should be able to continue. He needed help with anything more complicated, but that wouldn't be a problem. He had friends in the village.

He grinned at the wall like an idiot. He did have friends, and they were all part of this clan now. In his life, both before he became a hunter and after, he could never have imagined he'd be a clan member. He was human, and there was nothing special about him, yet Clay and Rowan had decided to take him in. He was safer than he'd been in years, and no one was yelling at him to fight like a man, like in that *Disney* movie.

He snorted at the thought of Cornelius shirtless and with long hair. It didn't fit, and Cornelius was much more cruel than the guy in the movie—and not nearly as handsome. Luckily, Chris would never have to deal with him again.

Thank God for small mercies.

His phone vibrated on the kitchen counter, and he put down his paintbrush to see who it was. It could be Rowan or Clay with orders to gather so they could go kick Kudlak ass. In that case, Chris would have to be quick leaving the house. Luckily, it wasn't them, and Chris's smile widened as he answered the call. "Ronnie," he exclaimed.

There was a pause before his childhood best friend answered. "You sound happy."

His words made Chris feel guilty. "I'm okay, I guess. What about you?"

Ronnie sighed. "I didn't mean that you had to stop being happy or apologize."

"I didn't apologize."

"You might as well have. I *want* you to be happy, Chris. It makes me feel better about you joining the hunters." He sighed again. "I wish you would come home. I miss you."

Chris closed his eyes and leaned his hip against the kitchen counter. He had so many feelings when it came to Ronnie that it was hard to make sense of them.

Ronnie was his childhood best friend. They'd grown up together, and they'd had each other's backs. They'd seen each other every day until the night they'd been attacked by a Kudlak.

They'd both survived. Chris was pretty sure that

sometimes Ronnie wished he hadn't, but even though he was scarred, he was alive. That was all Chris cared about, but it wasn't all *Ronnie* cared about.

Chris had thought that by joining the hunters, he'd make Ronnie happy that someone was avenging him and making the world a safer place, but he didn't think he'd succeeded, at least not entirely. He suspected Ronnie was still angry at him for leaving him behind, and he didn't blame him. They'd promised each other they'd always be together, but Chris had left, and Ronnie hadn't been able to follow.

But things were different now. Ronnie didn't know all of it, but it was time to tell him so he could make a decision Chris had known was coming for a while now.

He pushed away from the counter and flopped into one of the chairs at the kitchen table. "I miss you, too. Maybe you could come visit," he offered.

"You know I can't." Ronnie's voice was small, something Chris didn't think he could ever associate with his friend.

Ronnie had always been bigger than life. He'd been popular and open and had always had a smile on his lips. Everyone loved him. Knowing what he'd become because of the attack made Chris's heart ache, but he knew from experience there was nothing he could do about it. He couldn't help Ronnie where he was now. Ronnie himself was the only one who could do anything, but Chris could gently push him along.

"No, I don't know that you can't. I know you feel that your house is the only place you can be safe, but I told you about the village the last time I called, didn't I?"

"The village where you live with Krsniks?"

"They're good people. They were literally born to kill Kudlaks, so you'll never have to worry about that or them hurting you. We also have more people arriving daily who can help with the magic surrounding the village, so it's definitely safer than your apartment. It's only going to get safer once we get more of those people."

Chris couldn't say he understood everything Rowan had explained about Krsniks and their traditions, but he did know that some of the people who'd recently arrived had magic powers or something. They could create wards and keep the village safe while the Krsniks hunted the Kudlaks. Rowan had said that was how things had always been, and he wanted the village to be safe.

Everyone did. This was their safe haven, the only place where they could be sure the Kudlaks wouldn't get to them. Here, Ronnie would never have to worry about them.

"Besides, we're also under the protection of the Whitedell pride," Chris added, knowing Ronnie had heard of them.

Who hadn't? Their alpha was part of the council that had been created more than a decade earlier, and he barely looked any older than he had back then. Everyone had been shocked by the knowledge that shifters existed, but Chris had always thought it was cool. He still did. He was human, and he'd never be anything else, but that was fine with him. He didn't need to be anything else, especially when he could do what he had to as he was.

As long as he could fight Kudlaks and protect the people he cared about, he was happy.

"Have you met their alpha?" Ronnie asked.

"Not in person, but he's visited the village a few times. I did meet several pride members, though. There's one especially that I'm sure you would get along with. He has pink hair and more piercings than I've ever seen on anyone."

"Maybe I *should* visit," Ronnie said.

Chris told himself not to hope too much. It wouldn't be the first time Ronnie said he wanted to join him only to change his mind or realize he couldn't.

He'd been stuck in his apartment for years now. He was terrified of leaving the only place where he felt safe, and Chris understood that. It was why he'd been trying to make the world a safer place. He wanted Ronnie to be able to live his life the way he deserved.

The village was safe. Ronnie would still be afraid, but it was time for him to start living his life again, and Chris couldn't think of a better place to do so. Moving here wouldn't be enough for him to get over his fears, but it would be the first step, and that might be all he needed.

That, and to talk to a therapist, but Ronnie had always refused. Even though everyone knew about the paranormal world, Ronnie still didn't want to talk about the Kudlak who had attacked him. The only person who knew everything was Chris, but only because he'd been there. No matter how much Chris wanted to help Ronnie, he wasn't sure he could.

"Think about it," he said, aware that he sounded like he was begging. "We have more Krsniks arriving every day, along with the Vila, who take care of the magical part of the village's protection. The Whitedell pride is so close that if we need anything, they're here in minutes. I know thinking about that much change is scary, but this is the safest place on earth, and I don't want you to say no to coming until you've really thought about it."

Chris didn't expect anything to change, so he was surprised by Ronnie's answer.

"I'm not making any promises, but I'll think about it."

That was all Chris wanted.

Gary loved his new house. He didn't feel like he deserved it, but that was an entirely different problem.

Everyone he loved was dead. They'd been killed, had their lives cut short, and he'd stood there, not doing anything. He'd always thought he should have died with them, and he still did. That was why he didn't deserve this place. He should be long gone now, yet here he was.

He shook his head. No matter how guilty he felt about not doing more when his village was attacked, he could hear his parents' voices scolding him in his mind. His mother especially would be pissed if she found out he was thinking of himself like that. She wouldn't want him to feel guilty for something he'd had no power over. Even if he had fought the Kudlaks, he would have died with his family and the rest of the village. He wouldn't have been able to stand up to the Kudlaks.

He still wouldn't be able to, even today. The fact that he and the other Vila he'd joined had been on the run from a group of Kudlaks pointed to that. Gary had tried fighting them off, but Dermot had dragged him away, and he'd been right to do so. That time around, too, Gary would have died if the Kudlaks had come close enough.

He balled his hands up into fists but resisted the urge to punch the wall. It wouldn't hurt anyone but himself. It certainly wouldn't hurt any Kudlaks.

Gary despised them. He despised what they did, the way they destroyed families and villages, the way they'd been hunting Krsniks and Vila for decades. Gary had lost everything, and he'd been on the run for years because of them.

But he wasn't anymore.

He looked around his tiny yard, smiling at the thought that he could grow herbs and plants. It would take some time and work before he could, because the village had been abandoned a while ago and everything was overgrown and crumbling down, but he didn't mind. Working hard would make the place feel more like his.

As long as he could let go of the guilt, anyway.

And the fear. It was always present, even though he was safe in the village. They could be safer, though, and knowing that bothered Gary. His role was to use his magic to protect the Krsniks and their families in the village, but he wasn't enough. There weren't enough Vila here for now, which meant the protective ward around the village wasn't as strong as it should be. *That* meant there was a chance the Kudlaks would find and attack them, and if that happened, Gary would need to be ready.

He wouldn't run this time. He wouldn't hide. He wouldn't lose another village and another group of people he cared about. If the Kudlaks attacked, Gary would fight them.

Which was a problem because he had no idea how to fight. Kudlaks were strong and fast. The only beings capable of holding their own against them were the Krsniks, who'd been born to do so. Gary would never be a Krsnik, but maybe he didn't have to be. It wasn't like he had to kill every Kudlak in the world—although that was tempting. He just had to be able to fight them off if they attacked the village, and he believed that was entirely doable.

His mouth went dry at the thought of fighting a Kudlak. They'd decimated his family, had erased his village from the surface of the earth, and had been hunting him ever since. There wasn't a day in his life in which he hadn't thought about Kudlaks and hadn't been afraid.

He wasn't sure he could ever get over that.

He wanted to. He finally had a place to call home again, and he was ready to do anything in his power to defend it. That meant having someone who knew what they were doing teach him to fight. He would never expect to defeat a Kudlak, but if he could hold them back until the Krsniks arrived, he'd consider that good enough.

He didn't know the fighters in this village yet, but there was one person he could ask. Alexis had been part of the same village and the same clan as Gary. They'd both lost everyone they cared about. In fact, they'd each believed the other had died, too, and had only recently found out they were alive.

They hadn't lost their entire clan. They still had each other, and that counted for something. Hopefully that would be enough to convince Alexis to give Gary self-defense lessons.

Gary stood where he was in the center of his yard for a moment longer. He tilted his head toward the sky, enjoying the heat of the June sun on his skin. It was too late in the year to plant many of the things he wanted to grow, but he had a list, and by this time next year, he'd have the yard exactly the way he wanted it.

He couldn't wait.

He couldn't remember the last time he'd been so excited about something. It had probably been when he'd still lived with his old clan. After they'd been killed, his entire focus had been on surviving, and that didn't leave much time to dream. When he did dream, all he saw was blood and pain, and that wasn't what he wanted, either. He'd been there when the village had been attacked. He didn't need to be reminded of what had happened that day. He'd lived it on his own skin, even though he'd survived.

After enjoying the sun for a few more moments, Gary decided he needed to stop wasting time. He was afraid of what Alexis would say when he asked for help, but he hoped Alexis would consider the fact that they'd both belonged to the same clan before. Besides, he wanted the village to be safe as much as Gary did. It would be safer if Gary and the other Vila could defend themselves. Alexis hadn't argued about the humans going on raids, so why should he about this?

Gary was about to find out.

He was nervous as he went to look for his friend, but not so much so that he didn't notice how much the village was changing day by day. Everyone had been assigned their own home if that was what they wanted. Gary had said yes right away when he'd been offered one, but he was starting to wonder if he should have waited. He didn't need an entire house to himself, even though there were plenty of them, and the only payment the clan wanted was for the new owners to fix them up. He felt he didn't deserve it and that he should suffer for what he hadn't been able to do in the past, even though he knew he was the only one who felt that way. He didn't think Alexis did, even though the village had been his, too.

Over the years, Gary had realized that guilt was the hardest emotion to let go of. He could ignore fear and sadness but not guilt. Every time he did something that made him realize he was still alive, he thought about the people who weren't. He thought about how *they* should be the ones enjoying this life. Maybe they would be if he'd been more capable of defending them.

He shook his head. Thinking about that wouldn't help. It never had.

He debated going to Alexis's house, then decided that first he'd go to the training area. It was there that most of the humans and Krsniks spent their day, so he wasn't surprised to see the place was crowded. The leaders of the clan, Rowan and Clay, were talking about building a gym or renovating one of the bigger buildings for that purpose, but for now, it was warm enough for everyone to train in the open.

Alexis was there, talking with another Krsnik at the edge of the wide area. She was nodding at something Alexis was saying, and when she looked up, she noticed Gary staring at them. She winked, flustering him. Thankfully, he didn't have to wait long. Alexis looked up and saw him, too, and after saying something else to his friend, he came toward Gary.

Gary sucked in a breath. This was it. He just had to say the right words, and Alexis would have to let him learn how to defend himself.

And the people they both cared about.

Ronnie hadn't decided to move to the village yet, which meant Chris could still influence his decision. No matter how many times Chris told his friend that the village was safe, he didn't think Ronnie would believe it until he saw it with his own two eyes. If he ever visited, Chris would have to convince him to stay, which was why Chris needed to make the village even safer.

How was he supposed to do that?

He hoped Boyd and Alexis would have answers to that question. He was headed to their house for dinner, and he was excited about it. He and Boyd had lived in the same warehouse before. They'd stuck together, along with Kendrick. It had been the only way for them to survive, both during fights with Kudlaks and in the warehouse with the other hunters. Many of them had been even more vicious than the Kudlaks, something Chris hadn't thought possible after seeing what some of them had done.

But now, the three of them lived in different houses. It felt good to have privacy and space, but Chris also missed their closeness. For years, they'd been in each other's pockets, but now, those pockets were empty.

Luckily, the three of them lived in the village, which meant they could see each other as often as they wanted. It was a little more complicated with Boyd, since he'd met his mate and lived with Alexis now, but Chris liked Alexis. He didn't care that Alexis was a Krsnik, even though they were scarily similar to Kudlaks.

They had to be to defeat them.

As long as Boyd was happy, Chris wouldn't judge or care about what kind of being Alexis was, but he couldn't imagine allowing anyone to drink his blood.

He shuddered as he walked. He'd seen Ronnie's scars, and most of them were on his neck. The Kudlak who'd taken him had used him as a chew toy, drinking from him again and again without caring that he would eventually die from it. It was pure luck that Ronnie hadn't.

Chris would always feel guilty that the Kudlak had preferred his friend. He'd been knocked unconscious, and by the time he'd awakened, Ronnie had been wounded and almost drained of blood. The Kudlak hadn't believed Chris would be a danger, so he hadn't tied him, and Chris had managed to grab Ronnie and drag him away while the Kudlak was drunk on Ronnie's blood. He'd always associate blood drinking with that.

Boyd had lost his sister to Kudlaks, yet he didn't seem to have a problem allowing Alexis to drink from him. Chris supposed things were different because of who Alexis was to him. He wasn't just a Krsnik, and he definitely wasn't a Kudlak. He was Boyd's mate, and they were happy together. Of course Boyd was fine letting Alexis drink his blood.

Chris wondered if he'd ever be anyone's mate. It was possible. He lived in a village surrounded by paranormal beings, so it made sense that he might be the mate to one of them. So far, he hadn't met that person, but he was still young. He didn't need a mate. He was fine by himself.

He'd be fine as long as they didn't want to drink his blood. He hoped his mate wouldn't be a Krsnik, although he was sure that if they were, he'd accept it. He'd seen how happy Boyd was with Alexis, and he wanted the same for himself.

He reached Boyd's house after only a few minutes of walking and quickly knocked on the door. It was the first time for him to have dinner with them since Alexis had entered Boyd's life, but he knew Alexis well. He couldn't help but wonder how odd it would be to have dinner with a Krsnik. He knew Alexis could eat human food, but he also drank Boyd's blood. Was it something he'd want to do tonight?

The door swung open, and Boyd smiled at Chris. "Hey."

"Hey."

"I just wanted to warn you before you walked in," Boyd said, stopping Chris in his tracks.

"Warn me about what?"

"We have another guest for dinner. Alexis came home with him after training today, and I thought it wouldn't hurt anyone for him to stay. He's Alexis's friend from their old clan."

Chris had heard the story. He knew Alexis had lost his entire clan to Kudlaks, which wasn't an unusual story. The hunters had all lost someone because of the Kudlaks—sometimes a friend, other times a family member, and the worst times, their entire family. Chris couldn't imagine what it had been like for Alexis and his friend, and he was glad they'd found each other again.

"I don't have a problem with that."

Boyd beamed. "Great. Well, they're in the kitchen."

Chris looked around as he and Boyd made their way over. Boyd's house had been in disrepair, just like Chris's, but Boyd seemed to be better with his hands. Alexis had probably helped, too. The house wasn't finished, but it was well on its way, and it looked good.

"You're going to have to help me do the same back at my place," Chris said as he gestured at the newly repaired stairs. "I'm a little scared to go up and down the stairs because it feels like they might break anytime I do."

Boyd frowned. "Maybe you shouldn't use them, then."

"Probably not, but the bed is upstairs, and I spent too much time sleeping on the floor to want to do that again." Although even if he did, it would be very different from sleeping on the floor at the warehouse. At least his place was clean and warm.

He and Boyd stepped into the kitchen. Alexis was sitting at the island with his friend. They were both talking, but Alexis turned when Boyd walked past him. Boyd leaned down to kiss the top of Alexis's head as if it were a natural movement for them.

It was, and it made Chris yearn for the same.

"It's good to see you," Alexis said when Chris neared him.

"It is. Thank you for allowing me to come to dinner."

"You're Boyd's best friend. You can come over for dinner every day if you want."

Chris laughed. "I'd be careful what you offer me. You might never get rid of me."

Alexis's smile was easy. "I wouldn't offer if I didn't want you here." He turned toward his friend. "Chris, this is Gary. You were there when we rescued him and the other Vila from the Kudlaks hunting them. He was part of my old clan, but I don't think I introduced the two of you. Gary, this is Chris, Boyd's best friend."

Gary turned around in his seat. Knowing he was a Vila, Chris knew what to expect. From what he'd seen, most of them had blond hair and blue eyes and were incredibly beautiful. Gary wasn't an exception, but somehow, he seemed even more stunning than the other Vila Chris had seen around the village. Older, too, but Chris thought that was part of his charm.

He smiled and offered Gary his hand. "It's a pleasure to meet you."

Gary simply stared. His eyes were wide, and Chris had to resist the urge to look behind himself to check what Gary was staring at. He wasn't sure why the man was reacting to him like this, but it made him nervous.

He rubbed the back of his neck. "I'm sorry we didn't meet sooner. I guess we were both busy trying to survive those Kudlaks." Chris was pretty sure he would have remembered Gary if he'd noticed him that day. The people under attack had been whisked back to the village quickly, though, while Chris had stayed behind with the others to fight the Kudlaks.

Gary was still staring. Chris decided that meant he could stare, too. After all, Gary was a sight to behold.

Chris wasn't sure how aging worked for Vila, but most paranormal beings aged much slower than humans. Gary appeared to be in his early forties, which probably meant he was three hundred years old or something like that.

Chris almost snorted. Okay, maybe not three hundred, but definitely older than Chris, and not by just a few years.

"Anyway," Chris continued. "How have you been finding the village? It's new for me, too, although I lived with a bunch of hunters for a while. I guess that's why it's odd. I have my own place now." And he was babbling, which wasn't like him.

He turned to Boyd, who was looking at him, clearly amused. Chris resisted the urge to roll his eyes. He didn't know what to do to get an answer out of Gary, and he was starting to get worried. Did he have something on his face? Why was the man still staring without saying a word?

And why did it make Chris want to kiss him?

Gary knew he should say something. It was rude to stare and even more so not to participate in the conversation. Chris was trying to be nice, and here Gary was, staring at him like he'd seen a ghost.

He might as well have.

When Alexis had asked him to come to the house he shared with Boyd for dinner, Gary hadn't expected to find his mate there.

"Everything all right?" Alexis asked.

Gary finally snapped out of it. He cleared his throat and smiled at Chris, still unable to look away from him. At least he didn't look like a dead fish anymore. "Being in the village is nice. It's been a while since I felt this safe."

Chris visibly relaxed, probably because Gary wasn't freaking him out anymore. "Yeah, that's definitely a plus. I'm trying to convince my best friend to move here, but it's complicated."

"When isn't it?"

Gary didn't know what to do. Should he tell Chris he was his mate? How would Chris take it? Gary was pretty sure he was as human as Boyd, which meant he wouldn't know they were mates unless Gary told him.

Chris turned to Boyd, and Gary leaned back against the kitchen island. He needed the support if he didn't want to topple off the stool he was sitting on.

"Okay, it's clear something's happened, and I need to know what," Alexis said as he sat back down. He leaned close to Gary, cutting off Gary's view of Chris.

Gary leaned around Alexis. He wanted to look at his mate. He was very different from Gary, but Gary wouldn't have it any other way. He loved Chris's messy brown hair and his dark eyes. Chris was younger than Gary, but the difference in age didn't bother Gary, although it might bother Chris because Gary wasn't only older—he also *looked* older.

"You're freaking me out," Alexis warned.

Gary needed to stop it, because if Alexis was freaking out, Boyd would start doing the same, and it would become even more awkward.

Gary leaned forward and put a hand on Alexis's arm. "I'm fine. I promise that what's happening isn't a bad thing." Or at least, he didn't think it would be. It all depended on how Chris took the news.

Alexis narrowed his eyes. "You realize I'm not going to believe you just because you say it's not, right? You already surprised me when you asked about self-defense lessons. That's enough unexpected stuff from you for today."

Gary smiled. Alexis had been surprised, but like Gary had expected, he'd agreed to help him. "Chris really was there when you and the others rescued me?" he asked.

Alexis frowned, but thankfully, he answered without asking where Gary was going with his question. "He was. I'm not surprised you didn't notice him. It was a mess."

It had been, and it also had been dark, and Gary had been terrified. It had been chaos until he and the others had been shimmered to the village. Once here, they'd been taken care of. People had asked if they needed medical help and had shown them to one of the empty houses. Alexis had been there for Gary when he'd returned, but Gary didn't remember anyone else except for Boyd.

He couldn't believe his mate had been living a few houses down from his since he moved to the village and he hadn't known. He didn't even understand how it was possible. How had he never seen Chris around?

Asking himself those questions wouldn't change anything. Now, he *had* seen Chris, and he needed to decide what he wanted to do about it.

"What is it?" Alexis asked in a whisper. "Do you recognize Chris from somewhere? Did he hurt you in the past?"

Gary quickly shook his head. "Of course not. I'd never seen him until tonight."

"And seeing him was enough to shock you." Alexis's eyes widened. "Wait. I know that expression. You're in shock and overwhelmed, and I remember all too well how I felt when I met Boyd. Is that what's happening?"

Gary looked at Chris, but he was busy talking with Boyd. He glanced at Gary, then quickly away when he saw that Gary was looking at him. "It is," he confirmed.

Alexis leaned back. Gary wasn't sure how his friend would take the news. Maybe they weren't even friends anymore. They hadn't been close when they'd been part of the same clan, but they were the only ones left, and they shared a certain kinship. Maybe that wasn't enough for Alexis, though. He loved his mate, and he seemed protective of his mate's friends. He might think that Gary wasn't good enough for Chris.

Gary didn't think he was.

Chris was a hunter, and he deserved to be bonded to a fighter, someone who could protect him. He put his life in danger every time he left the village, especially because he didn't have anything more than his strength and ability against Kudlaks. He wasn't a Krsnik.

He could die so easily.

Gary shivered in horror. He didn't know if he could do this. How was he supposed to watch his mate leave the village time and time again to protect people, put himself in danger, and possibly never come back? How was Gary supposed to stay behind and accept it? He couldn't protect Chris. He couldn't do anything to help in the fight against the Kudlaks.

"You should tell him," Alexis finally said.

"I don't know. I'm not sure it's the right thing to do."

Chris seemed like a good person, which probably meant he'd give Gary a chance. He didn't know that Gary wasn't worth it. He didn't know that Gary had allowed his clan to be decimated. He'd run instead of fighting for his life and the lives of the people he loved.

Gary was glad to be part of a new clan, but he could never ignore the fear that he'd lose these people, too. With the Kudlaks more active than ever and attacking in groups, it was a possibility. Gary didn't think he could survive if it happened to him a second time. If it did, he'd fight to the death. He wouldn't abandon the people he cared about again.

He wouldn't abandon Chris.

"I know it's a lot, especially after everything else," Alexis murmured. "But at the very least, he deserves to know. Besides, I see you're working yourself up, and I don't think you have a reason to. Chris is a nice person. He's a reasonable guy. Don't give up on your relationship with him just because he's human and might not understand how important this is."

"That wouldn't be the reason," Gary said as he peeked at Chris again. "He deserves better."

Alexis got to his feet. "He should be the one deciding that." He turned to his mate. "I need to show you something outside."

Boyd frowned. "What?"

"Come on. I'll show you."

Boyd was clearly confused, but when Alexis held his hand out, he took it without hesitation. That was what their bond meant. They trusted each other with their lives.

But Chris could never trust Gary with his.

Boyd and Alexis quickly left, and Gary and Chris were alone. Chris was staring at Gary with his head cocked, probably trying to make sense of what was going on. "Something tells me Alexis didn't really have to show Boyd something," he said slowly.

"I don't think he did."

"Unless it was a code word for sex, but I don't think they'd do that with us here."

Gary's body flushed at the thought of sex, but it had nothing to do with Alexis and Boyd. He couldn't start thinking about sex with Chris, though. "They left us alone because there's something I need to tell you."

Chris moved closer and leaned against the kitchen island. He was in front of Gary now, separated from him only by the counter. "What is it?"

"Do you know much about my species?"

Chris shook his head. "You look a bit like a Nix, but I know you're not. You have blue eyes, for one, and while I haven't seen your ears, they don't look pointed."

Gary pushed his long hair away from his ears. "They're not. We have some things in common with Nix, but not a lot. One of those things is that we can identify our mates by sight."

Chris stared at Gary for so long that Gary wondered if he understood what he'd said.

"Okay," Chris eventually said. "You're going to have to be more specific, because I don't know if I can believe what I think you just told me."

Chris deserved for Gary to be completely honest. If he rejected Gary, it would hurt, but it might as well happen now that they barely knew each other.

Gary swallowed. "I'm saying that as soon as you walked into the room, I knew you were my mate."

Chapter Two

Chris was supposed to continue painting the kitchen walls, but he just stood there like an idiot. He had the brush in his hand and everything, but his focus was somewhere else entirely.

He huffed, dipped the brush into the paint again, and went to work.

He wasn't surprised that he couldn't focus. After all, he'd found out he was someone's mate. Having just told Boyd he didn't want a mate, he wasn't sure how to feel about it.

Did he *need* a mate? No. He was pretty sure most people didn't need someone like that in their life. Did he *want* a mate? That was an entirely different question.

Since he'd become a hunter, he'd avoided having relationships as much as he could. He hadn't always succeeded, but it hadn't been easy to trust the people he worked with. The last woman he'd been with had stayed with Cornelius and his hunters, and he'd realized that he hadn't known her as well as he'd thought he did. He hadn't expected her to continue following Cornelius, considering what Cornelius was doing and believed was right, and he hated that he'd been with her.

He couldn't change that. The only thing he could change was the future, but he had no idea what it would look like. What was he supposed to do with the knowledge that he was Gary's mate? He was Gary's only chance to have that kind of relationship, so he didn't want to dismiss it, and he wasn't completely opposed to being with Gary, but he didn't know the man. He also wasn't sure *he'd* be a good mate or boyfriend.

There was a way around him not knowing Gary. It wasn't like they were in a rush. After telling him he was his mate, Gary hadn't demanded they bond right away. He'd actually looked like he expected Chris to reject him, and while that wasn't what Chris had done, he'd panicked and left before dinner. Boyd had called him as he'd reached home, and Chris had reassured him that he was all right and just needed time, but he still didn't know what to do, and he'd had time — the entire night and this morning.

He'd gone to training this morning and had carefully avoided looking in Alexis's direction. Alexis was Gary's friend, and Chris didn't want to put him in an awkward situation. Boyd hadn't been there since he'd decided he didn't want to be a hunter anymore, so Chris hadn't needed to talk about his feelings. Kendrick had pushed to find out why Chris was so grumpy, but Chris had told him to fuck off, and Kendrick had let it go. Thankfully, he didn't get offended easily.

But Chris couldn't avoid people forever. He couldn't even avoid them for more than a day or two. The problem was that he didn't have answers to their questions.

He didn't even have answers to his own questions.

He needed to talk to Gary, but what was he supposed to tell him? He supposed that at the very least, he could explain he'd been in shock and had needed space. He was pretty sure Gary would give him time if he needed it, but Chris didn't want to lead him on. What if he eventually decided he didn't want a mate? What would Gary do?

But could he do that to him? Chris might be human, but he knew how important mates were to paranormal beings. He'd also seen how happy their mates were, even when they were humans. He just had to look at Boyd. He'd been fine before, but now that he was with Alexis, he never stopped smiling. Chris was glad to see his friend happy, but he had a hard time imagining himself in Boyd's place.

A knock on the door made him freeze. Was it Gary? Was he here to get an explanation of what had happened yesterday? If he was, he wouldn't get what he wanted because Chris didn't have an explanation beyond the fact that he'd freaked out.

He looked in the direction of the front door and wondered if he could ignore it. It might not be Gary, but Chris wasn't sure he wanted to take the risk. He wasn't ready to talk to the man. He didn't even know what he'd tell him when he did.

He stayed where he was, and the knocking stopped. He relaxed, thinking that whoever had been standing at his front door was gone, only to turn and find Boyd standing outside his kitchen window, glaring at him with his arms crossed over his chest. Chris yelped and dropped his brush, getting his t-shirt dirty with paint.

"You're an asshole," he called out.

The window was open, so Boyd heard him. "*I'm* an asshole? You're ignoring me and Kendrick."

"I didn't know it was you."

"You would have if you'd opened the door."

He was right, but Chris wouldn't give him the satisfaction of admitting that. "What are you doing here?"

"We came to help you paint your kitchen. Kendrick has snacks."

Chris narrowed his eyes. "Is that the only reason you're here?" He was pretty sure Boyd knew what was happening with Gary. Gary was friends with Alexis, and there was no way Alexis would keep this kind of secret from Boyd.

"Why? Is there something you need to tell me?" Boyd asked, arching a brow.

Chris rolled his eyes. "Come in," he said, resigned. It looked like he was going to have to talk about Gary whether he wanted to or not. Maybe it was a good thing. It might be what he needed to decide what he wanted to do.

Boyd left, and seconds later, Chris heard the front door open. He ignored it and looked down at his t-shirt, grimacing at the sight of the paint. Luckily, it was an older t-shirt, but he didn't own that many clothes, so he needed to be more careful.

"I thought you weren't in," Kendrick accused as he walked into the kitchen. He was carrying two bags and dropped both on the table.

"Sorry," Chris told him. "I didn't hear the knock."

"And I'm a Kudlak. Don't bullshit me. I might not be as confrontational as Boyd, but it doesn't mean I don't know when you're lying to me."

Chris pinched the bridge of his nose. "Why am I friends with the two of you again?"

Kendrick blew him a kiss. "Because you love us." He dropped onto one of the chairs at the table and dragged the bags closer. "Go wash up. We have a lot of talking to do." He looked around the room. "And even more painting."

Chris groaned but obeyed. There would be no getting out of this.

As he left the kitchen, his path crossed with Boyd's, who was checking the staircase. Chris remembered telling him about it, so he wasn't surprised. Boyd was good with his hands, and he wouldn't want Chris to get hurt.

"This needs work," Boyd said.

"I'm aware."

"Be careful when you use it."

"I always am. I thought you'd forbid me to continue using it."

"You'd still do it. You don't listen to people when you think you know better."

That much was true, and Chris could admit it. It wasn't a good personality trait, but he knew it was there, and he could work on fixing it. In this case, he had to use the stairs because his bed was on the second floor, as were his clothes.

As promised, he was careful as he climbed up. He thought about taking a shower, then decided that if the three of them were going to work on the house anyway, he shouldn't bother. He quickly washed up at the sink, then went back downstairs, not a bit surprised to see that Boyd and Kendrick had made themselves at home. They each had a beer, and Kendrick had opened a bag of chips.

Chris grabbed a beer from the fridge and flopped into one of the two remaining chairs at his table. He looked at his friends, once again stunned by the way everything had gone. It was hard to believe that after living in the hunters' warehouse for so long, he had a home where he could sit at the table with his friends.

"Boyd told me about Gary," Kendrick offered.

Chris grimaced. "I'm not surprised. I can't really focus on having a mate right now, though. I'm trying to convince my best friend to move to the village, and I don't think I'll be able to relax until Ronnie's here." It was an excuse, but it was also true.

Boyd frowned. "Have you told Gary that?"

Chris sighed. He wouldn't get out of this conversation, and he might as well be honest about all of it. Ronnie was his best friend, but Boyd and Kendrick were his friends, too. They might know what Chris should do.

And if they didn't, they could help him come up with a plan.

Even after Gary had been offered a home and a place in the village, he hadn't been sure he belonged here. He hadn't felt like he deserved to belong to a new village and clan, and he still didn't. He was sure he belonged here now, though. It didn't matter if he deserved it or not. His mate was here, which meant that Gary should be, too. If this weren't the right place for him, he wouldn't have found his mate here.

But knowing that he belonged didn't help. It made him feel slightly better but also more guilty. He wouldn't be able to defend these people if they were attacked. He'd lose everyone again if the Kudlaks found them.

But that wasn't his problem right now. No, his problem was that he had no idea what to tell his mate.

When Gary had told Chris that he was his mate yesterday evening, Chris had stared at him for a long time as if his brain was trying to make sense of what Gary had said. Gary understood how shocking the news was, so he'd let Chris be, and he'd done his best not to be offended when Chris had shakenly gotten up from his seat and run out the door. Gary couldn't think that Chris was horrified or afraid. He had to give him the benefit of the doubt and hope it was shock and awkwardness that had sent him running.

Not the thought of being Gary's mate.

Fate had brought Gary to the village. He didn't know what would happen if Chris didn't accept him as his mate, but he didn't think he could leave. That would hurt as much as losing everyone would, and maybe he deserved that, but he wouldn't survive it.

But maybe Chris did want him, and if he didn't now, maybe he would eventually. Gary had decided to give him time, but he also couldn't help but wonder if it would be a good idea to try and talk to him. The problem was that he didn't know Chris, and things between them were awkward. They wouldn't get better until they talked, but Gary didn't want Chris to feel like he was hounding him. There was no way for Chris to know that Gary didn't expect him to accept their bond right away until Gary told him, though.

Gary groaned and leaned back in the grass. He'd cleaned

up part of his yard this morning, needing something to focus on, but it hadn't helped. The yard was neater, but Gary's every thought was focused on Chris. He suspected that would continue for a while. He needed to find a way to fix what had happened yesterday, but he didn't know how. Would talking to Chris make him more comfortable or less? Would Chris feel like Gary was pushing if Gary tried telling him he wanted to give him time and get to know him?

Gary didn't know Chris well enough. He didn't know Chris at all. He had no idea how his mate would react to any conversation between them, but maybe there was someone he could ask.

He wiggled until he managed to get his hand in his back pocket, then took out his phone. It was new. Rowan, the clan leader, had gifted one to every Vila who'd arrived with Gary. Gary had never needed a phone. He'd never had anyone to call, which was sad. Now, though, his phone had numbers saved into it.

Including Alexis's number.

That was who Gary selected and called. He didn't know who else to talk to. He supposed he could tell Dermot or one of the others he'd been on the run with, but even though they were friendly, they weren't exactly friends. They'd banded together to survive, and they'd done what was necessary in order to do that, but while they'd been close, it didn't mean that Gary could trust them with this.

But he could trust Alexis. He was sure of that.

"I knew you'd call," Alexis said when he answered.

"I'm that predictable?"

"No, but you know Chris is Boyd's best friend. You're probably not comfortable enough to call Boyd, but me? You are."

Gary smiled at the sky. It was endlessly blue, so much so that he felt he could lose himself staring at it. Maybe it would help him stop obsessing over his mate.

He doubted anything could achieve that.

"I just need to know he's all right. I don't know how he took the news yesterday, but considering he ran from me, I think I can say it wasn't well," Gary explained.

"Why don't you come over? Boyd left, so I'm alone at the house. We can sit down and talk."

Gary sat up. "I don't want to bother you."

"You're not bothering me. Come on. I'll get lunch together, and we can eat as we talk." Alexis hesitated. "You don't have to talk about Chris if you're not comfortable with that. I realize we weren't best friends before, and we don't have to be now, but I thought I'd lost every member of my clan. Finding out you were still alive was a shock, and I feel we should get to know each other better. I love the new clan we have, but I don't want to forget about the old one."

Gary's chest squeezed. He couldn't believe that Alexis didn't hold what had happened against him, not even a little. Gary wouldn't have been able to defeat all the Kudlaks who'd attacked their clan, and he would have died along with the rest of the clan members if he'd tried, but the guilt was always strong. Even though he knew it wasn't logical, he felt that everyone had died because of him.

Alexis didn't seem to think that. He wanted to be Gary's friend, and Gary wanted the same.

"I'll come," he said.

"Good. The food won't be elaborate, but I suspect you already know that."

Gary did, and he didn't mind. The village was still tiny, and while Whitedell was close, it felt like most people here were wary of leaving the village to go and get groceries. They did because they didn't have a choice, but things would be much better once the village had a small grocery store.

Maybe Gary could take care of it. He'd never owned a store

before, but he'd need a job. He loved tending to his yard and being a healer, but he wanted to contribute to the village's life more.

"Whatever you have is perfect," he promised.

After he and Alexis hung up, he went to clean up and headed out. The sun was warm on his skin, and he looked around as he walked down the path. He could hear people in the houses as he walked past, the sound of a hammer and a saw. He could smell fresh paint and wood in the wind.

The village was coming together. It would take time for it to be like Gary's old village, but Gary didn't mind. He liked feeling like he was starting something new, maybe giving himself a fresh beginning. He hadn't been born in this clan, but that didn't mean he wasn't part of it. His mate was here, which meant Gary was supposed to be here, too.

He'd help the village, one way or another. Alexis had agreed to give him self-defense lessons, but it would be a while before Gary could be helpful against an attacker, especially a Kudlak. That wasn't the only means he had to be useful to the village, and he decided he would talk to the two clan leaders about the grocery store. He suspected most clan members would feel relieved if they had a store in the village. It wouldn't be as big as the stores in Whitedell, so it wouldn't hold as many varieties of food, but it might still be enough. At the very least, it would mean people wouldn't have to go all the way to Whitedell if they only needed a few things.

Gary could do this. He could build himself a new life here and protect it if he had to. He had even more incentive this time around.

He had his mate.

Chris took a sip of his beer. "No, I haven't told Gary. I haven't talked to him at all since yesterday evening."

Kendrick rolled his eyes. "And how do you suppose you'll find a solution? You can't do it on your own this time, Chris. Gary is as involved as you are. It's not fair to shut him out."

Chris groaned and rubbed his face. "I'm not shutting him out. I just need time." Gary probably understood, right? He had to know how much of a shock the news was to Chris. He probably hadn't expected Chris to run away, but Chris's reaction was understandable, wasn't it?

"I'm not going to say what I did yesterday evening was fair, but it's the only thing I could do," Chris explained. "And I know I need to talk to him. I promise I will."

"But you want to move your friend to the village first," Boyd offered.

"It's not that I want to do it first. I'm just worried about Ronnie." Chris hesitated. The three of them had talked about the reasons they'd become hunters before, but Chris had never gone into details. None of them had. Maybe his friends would understand more easily why he was so worried about Ronnie if he gave them more.

He rolled his beer bottle between his palms as he tried to find the right way to say this. He didn't think there was one. He just had to say the words.

"I hate that I couldn't help Ronnie when we were taken. I don't know if the Kudlak thought I was dead or if he was keeping me for dessert, but he didn't bite me. I'd lain there, unconscious while Ronnie was tortured and drained almost to the point of death."

"You saved him," Boyd said gently.

"I guess I did. I dragged him out of that place and back home, and I took care of him as well as I could, but he went through hell. He's been stuck in his apartment since he moved in there. When he was still with his parents, at least he talked to them and saw someone every day, but now he's completely alone. I don't think he's left the place for years. I call him as

29

often as I can, but it's not the same, and he deserves to stop feeling like he's in danger. He deserves to be safe and know that people will protect him if anything happens. He needs to know that I won't allow another Kudlak to hurt him ever again. I can't promise that if he stays in his apartment, but I can promise he'll be safer here in the village."

"Maybe so, but it's not something you can decide for him," Kendrick said gently. "We all have trauma in our lives. We all deal with it in different ways. This is how Ronnie has decided to deal with it."

"But that's the thing. He's not dealing with it. He's hiding, and the years are passing. I only ever wanted him to be happy, and I thought that by showing him I could kill Kudlaks, he'd know I could protect him. I wanted to bring him the head of the Kudlak who'd hurt him, but I never saw the monster again. I think it's time to let go of that, but I'm never letting go of Ronnie. If he comes here, he'll be protected. He'll never have to worry about what will happen to him again."

"But it might also put him in the line of fire," Boyd pointed out. "We're trying to make the village as safe as possible, but there are still so few of us that someone might slip in."

"But if Ronnie were here, I wouldn't feel as helpless as I do now. I'd be able to protect him better, and even though there are so few members of the clan right now, more people are starting to arrive. I have faith in Clay and Rowan. I truly believe this is the safest place from the Kudlaks Ronnie could live at."

Boyd nodded. "Well, you can't force him, but you can try to convince him."

"How? I've tried already, but he's stubborn and scared."

Which was understandable. Chris was afraid, too, even though he hadn't gone through what Ronnie had been through. He was always terrified when he went out on hunts, but he'd learned to live with that feeling and to use it to his advantage. Ronnie would never be a hunter, but that didn't mean he had to be a recluse in his apartment. If Ronnie moved to the village, he could make friends, go to the grocery store, take walks, and go back to a mostly normal life.

Boyd grinned. "What would Ronnie do if he knew you'd found your mate but haven't even talked to him?"

Chris didn't even have to think to know the answer to that question. "He'd kick my ass for not at least telling Gary I need time."

"And how can he kick your ass from where he is?"

Chris leaned back in his chair. There was no way to know if this would be a good enough reason to get Ronnie to leave his apartment, but it wouldn't hurt to try. Besides, Chris wanted to tell him about Gary. Ronnie had always been the smarter of the two of them, so he'd know what Chris was supposed to do. He wouldn't let Chris hide and be stubborn about any of this. He'd forced him to treat Gary the right way, something Chris should really start doing on his own.

He would. He didn't know what he wanted from Gary or what he had to offer, but he wouldn't reject him. He had no idea if things could work between them, but rejecting him felt harsh and cruel. Gary was a Vila, and Chris was his mate. The least he could do was get to know him before he decided things could or couldn't work between them.

Kendrick mirrored Boyd's grin and leaned forward. "Call him and put him on speaker. I always wanted to meet him, and I can't wait to hear what he has to say about the mess you made with Gary."

Chris rolled his eyes, but if Ronnie was going to move here, he might as well get to know Boyd and Kendrick now. He was sure the three of them would get along. They all shared at least one thing.

They knew how stubborn Chris was.

He grabbed his phone from the kitchen table and pulled up

Ronnie's number. He hesitated, then went for a regular phone call rather than a video call. He didn't know if Ronnie would want Kendrick and Boyd to see him.

"Twice in two days? What's going on in that village of yours?" Ronnie asked when he answered.

Chris grinned. "To be fair, you called me yesterday."

"I didn't think anything would happen so quickly after my phone call. What's going on?" Ronnie paused. "Are you calling to try to convince me to move?"

"I'm calling to introduce you to two of my closest friends here. Boyd and Kendrick, say hello to Ronnie."

Both of them obeyed. Kendrick was smiling like an idiot, while Boyd seemed amused. It was a pity Chris couldn't see Ronnie's expression. He could read his best friend so well that he would have known what Ronnie was thinking.

"It's good to meet the two of you," Ronnie said. "But I don't understand what's going on."

"Well, I was talking to Boyd and Kendrick, and you came up. Something happened yesterday evening. They convinced me to call you so I could tell you right away, and since they were here, I decided I might as well introduce the three of you."

"Stop making me worry and tell me what's going on. You're going to make me think the worse."

"Sorry," Chris quickly said. "That's the last thing I want."

Ronnie sighed. "I know. Just tell me."

"I think you'll want to visit the village soon because I want you to meet someone."

"Your two friends?"

"Not them. I met my mate yesterday evening."

Alexis was smiling when he opened the door after Gary knocked. That helped Gary relax—Alexis wouldn't be smiling if he didn't want him there.

Gary realized he needed to stop thinking that he wasn't welcome here and that Alexis blamed him for what had happened to their clan. He didn't. He'd been clear about that, and he was happy that Gary had survived. It was only the two of them now, and Gary didn't want to lose Alexis, especially not because he was an idiot and overthinking everything.

"Come in. I have leftovers from yesterday evening, if that's all right with you. Or I can make sandwiches," Alexis offered.

"Whatever's less bothersome for you."

"Let's reheat the leftovers, then."

Alexis had made pasta with tomato sauce yesterday, and Gary expected him to shove it in the microwave and call it a day. Instead, when he walked into the kitchen, he saw that Alexis had taken out a pan. Alexis gestured at the kitchen island, and Gary slid onto one of the stools as he watched Alexis open the fridge and take out the leftovers and butter. He put some of the butter into the pan and turned the heat on under it, then turned to Gary.

"Boyd is Chris's best friend, or at least one of them," he explained. "But I haven't lived here very long. I know Boyd's friends because they're important to Boyd, but Chris and I aren't close, so I'm not sure how helpful I can be. You should probably talk to Boyd."

Gary crossed his arms and sighed. "I might have to talk to him if Chris doesn't open up to me, but for now, I'm not sure anyone can help me."

Alexis spread the melted butter into the pan, then took the pasta leftovers and opened the container. It had been tasty yesterday, and Gary was sure it would be today, too. The tomato sauce had been delicious, and it had reminded him that it had been a long time since he'd eaten something he'd cooked for himself. Even now that he had his own home, he was often invited by Dermot and the other people he'd been on the run with. They'd become kind of a family, even though not all of them were close. Their closeness had been caused by being on the run and fear, and it was hard to let go of that and create a new basis for their relationship.

But Gary wanted to start cooking. He wanted to settle down in his new life. Before, he'd thought he didn't deserve it, so he'd kept himself ready to leave at any moment. Now, he wasn't sure where to start because eventually he hoped he'd have to include Chris in his decisions.

But that would come later.

Alexis dropped the pasta into the pan. The butter sizzled, and Gary's stomach growled.

"What I can help you with is the beginning of your relationship with your mate. I just went through it, and I find that the most important thing is communication," Alexis said as he moved the pasta around, spreading it until it covered the entire pan. He put down the wooden spoon and fully turned toward Gary. "You haven't talked to him yet, have you?"

"I want to, but I don't know if I should. It's clear from how he reacted yesterday that he needs time and space, and I want to give him that."

"Understandable, and I'm sure you need the same. My advice is to not let him put too much space between the two of you. We both know that obsessing over things doesn't help. It only warps your thoughts and makes you see what happened differently, and it's not easy to ignore it. I don't think you want Chris to ignore the fact that the two of you are mates."

"Of course not." But the thought of talking to Chris was terrifying. What if he didn't want to be Gary's mate? What if he rejected him?

But what if he welcomed him?

Gary would have to take a chance. It wasn't easy, but it wasn't the first time he'd done it. He'd taken a chance trusting

Dermot while he was running from Kudlaks. He'd been right to, and he was glad he had. The decision to talk to Chris was just as life-changing as the decision to trust Dermot, but in a different way. He wasn't risking his life.

Just his happiness.

"Then talk to him," Alexis said before grabbing the wooden spoon again.

The pasta was delicious this time around, too. Warming it in the butter had created a nice crust, and topped with grated cheese, it was the most delicious thing Gary had eaten in a long time, even better than it had been the night before. Gary liked it so much that he asked Alexis to explain what he'd done to make it, then decided to fix dinner for Chris. Chris hadn't eaten Alexis's pasta yesterday evening, and Gary's was bound to be different, but it would be a way to start a conversation.

The recipe wasn't complicated, and luckily, Gary had all the ingredients at home. Between that and taking care of his yard, the afternoon hours flew by, and soon enough he found himself walking to Chris's house. Alexis had told him which one it was, and Gary hoped Chris wouldn't mind him appearing on his doorstep without warning. He could easily have gotten Chris's number from Alexis or Boyd and asked him if this was all right, but he suspected that Chris would have tried to avoid him. If he was still freaking out, he might not want to see Gary.

Once he stood in front of the door, Gary sucked in a breath and quickly knocked before he could change his mind. He waited, shifting from one foot to another, hugging the dish with the pasta to his chest. It was warm, and he hoped Chris would open soon.

He did, then stood there, blinking at Gary. Gary raised the dish and smiled. "I'm sorry to bother you, but I cooked dinner, and I thought we could share. It's not Alexis's pasta, but I hope it'll be good anyway."

He waited, half expecting his mate to tell him to leave. Instead, Chris smiled and stepped to the side. "That smells delicious."

"I hope it is. I haven't cooked in a long time."

Chris closed the door and led Gary deeper into the house. "I can't imagine you had many opportunities to cook while you were on the run," he said.

"I didn't," Gary confirmed. "But I should get back to it. I enjoy cooking." Especially if he cooked for more than himself.

They settled at the kitchen table after Chris grabbed plates and silverware.

Gary dished out the pasta, and for a moment, they both ate in silence. It was the third meal in a row—except for breakfast—that he'd eaten pasta, but he didn't mind. He enjoyed it, although maybe tomorrow he'd eat a salad.

"I'm sorry I left so quickly yesterday evening," Chris said eventually.

Gary put down his fork. It was hard to make himself vulnerable, but he had to. It was the only way to get answers to his questions. "I understand why you did. It was a shock to you as much as it was to me, and I want to make things clear. I understand that you're human and probably didn't expect to be someone's mate, and I can give you all the time and space you need. I just need to know if you're willing to give this a chance. I don't want to hope only for you to tell me you don't want a mate in a week or a month."

To Gary's surprise, Chris set down his fork to cup Gary's cheek. The touch was startling but not unpleasant. Chris's hand was warm and slightly rough, as if he worked a lot with his hands. Looking around the house, Gary could imagine that he did. It was clear he was renovating the place himself.

"As I said earlier, I'm sorry I ran out," Chris said. "I was in shock, and I didn't know how to deal with it. I needed time to think about what you said, and that was enough for me to make a few decisions."

Gary's heart raced. "Yes?"

"I have a lot on my plate right now. I'm a hunter, of course, and I'm trying to convince my best friend to move to the village. That doesn't mean I don't want you. I just feel like this is a lot, but I do want to get to know you. I'm just not sure that rushing into anything will help."

"But you want to get to know me."

"I do, and I'm sure that eventually we'll feel it's time to bond and all of that. But like you said, I'm human, and I'm used to dating people before taking big steps like moving in with them. I know supernatural beings often don't date, but if it's okay with you, that's what I'd like to do."

It was more than Gary had expected, so he found it easy to smile. "We can date," he confirmed.

That was all he needed—a chance to show Chris that he could be the perfect mate for him and that they'd work well together. Fate had chosen this man for Gary, and he had no intention of giving him up or giving up on the bond they shared. He didn't care how long it took Chris to deal with his hang-ups and to feel he was ready for more.

Gary would take whatever Chris was willing to give him. Besides, Chris wasn't wrong. This was a lot for both of them, and it was best to take things slow.

As long as they gave each other a chance, Gary was sure everything would work out.

CHAPTER THREE

Chris felt like he was letting down the men in his life. There were two right now that he didn't know how to deal with, so he'd just been waiting to see what would happen. It didn't feel like enough. He wanted results, and while he could continue waiting and see what happened, maybe it was time to be more proactive.

He stared at his phone further down the kitchen table as he finished his breakfast. Ronnie had been happy for him when he told him he'd met his mate, but he hadn't made any promises about coming, not even to visit. Chris had been so sure he would that it had hit him hard. He'd isolated himself for a few days, licking his wounds and trying to come up with another excuse to get Ronnie to move. That meant he'd been neglecting his friends, but also Gary.

That wasn't fair to Gary. Gary had agreed to give Chris the time he needed, and Chris was grateful, but he also felt like a child throwing a temper tantrum. He needed to stop being an idiot, accept the truth, and move on.

He couldn't force Ronnie to do anything. As much as he wanted his best friend to join him at the village, Ronnie was the only one who could make the kind of decision that was needed for that to happen. Chris had asked him to come. He'd told him he'd be welcome and that he'd be safe, and he'd promised that no one would have anything against him becoming a clan member. He'd even gone as far as talking to Clay to be sure, and Clay had seemed happy at the thought of having more clan members.

That was all Chris could do. Ronnie would have to take the next step, and while Chris would support him, this was where his role ended when it came to his best friend. It hurt to accept it, but he had to.

There was nothing he could do about Ronnie, but there was something he could do about Gary. Gary had kept his distance because he was keeping his promise of giving Chris time, but Chris had enough of that and of his own behavior. If he wanted things to change, he needed to initiate those changes. He felt he was finally ready to do so. Hopefully Gary would forgive him for making a mess of this situation. Chris didn't know if he wanted to be with Gary yet, but the way Gary treated him made him at least want to try.

He'd said he wanted to get to know Gary, and he still did. That wouldn't happen if they didn't talk.

After breakfast, Chris quickly cleaned up the kitchen. He wasn't training this morning, so he'd slept in and had a lazy morning, and he felt he had more energy than he'd had in a long time. He was almost bouncing on his feet as he left his house. He had plans, and he couldn't wait.

He knew where Gary lived because Boyd had told him. As he walked there, he wondered if Gary had talked to Alexis about him. Gary had only recently arrived at the village, and while he had the friends he'd arrived with, they didn't know Chris. Alexis did, albeit not well. The meshing of different groups and people together to make up a new clan took a lot of effort and could sometimes be odd, but it was working. Eventually the clan would start to become more cohesive, and Chris couldn't wait to see what that would be like.

Even before becoming a hunter, he hadn't had a lot of people. His parents were better not thought of, and while he'd had Ronnie, that was pretty much it. Ronnie had been the one who had a lot of friends and people around him, but not Chris. Chris had been fine staying in Ronnie's shadow and having only his best friend.

It had been a hard choice to leave him behind. After the attack, Ronnie had done his best to go back to a normal life, but he'd failed. When Chris had seen that, he'd decided that he needed to help, but he hadn't known how. He'd stumbled on the hunters by accident by talking too much while he was drunk in a bar one night, and the rest was history. He'd left Ronnie behind to show him that he could defend him and make the world a better place, but he wasn't sure he'd succeeded. Ronnie was still stuck in his apartment, afraid of the world, not really living. Chris hated to think of him like that, but he'd done everything he could. Ronnie needed to take the next steps.

Chris hoped he would.

He stopped walking when he reached what he hoped was Gary's house. It was smaller than his, and the yard was in a much better shape. He wasn't surprised. He could easily imagine Gary tending to the yard, and he knew something about Vila's healing abilities. They weren't like Nix, so they used herbs and what nature gave them, but it worked damn well.

Before knocking on the door, Chris took out his phone. He pulled up Ronnie's number, quickly typed in a message, and sent it. He didn't write anything new. He just reassured Ronnie that he'd be there for him, whatever happened, and he hoped Ronnie would find a way to at least visit the village. Chris wouldn't bother him about it anymore. Ronnie knew what he wanted. There was no reason to push him into something he didn't.

When that was done, there was nothing to waste time on anymore. Chris stared at the little house again, cocking his head. It needed renovations, like his, but being here made him wonder if it was worth it to continue renovating his house. He and Gary were mates. That meant that eventually they would move in together, right? Where would they move? Which house would they choose?

Luckily, that wasn't a question Chris needed to answer now. He quickly knocked, then stepped back to wait for Gary to arrive. When he did, his cheeks were red, as if he'd been in the sun. He looked gorgeous and healthy, and for a moment, Chris could only stare at him.

"Chris. I wasn't expecting you," Gary said as he smoothed down his t-shirt.

It was dirty at the seam. There was also a trace of dirt on Gary's cheek that Chris wanted to clean or maybe kiss.

Chris didn't know what was happening to him. He'd told himself he needed time and space from Gary so he could make his decision about their relationship without influences, but maybe that wasn't how things worked. Maybe he was supposed to be influenced by his mate.

Chris didn't know much about the mating bond, just what most humans knew, so everything was new to him. He could probably ask Gary or even Boyd, but he felt this was something he needed to make sense of on his own.

He smiled at Gary. "I have the morning free, so I thought we could spend it together."

Gary stepped aside to let him in. "Of course. I'm sure you have many questions, and I'm ready to answer all of them."

Gary was trying to make himself useful, but that wasn't what Chris wanted. As he followed him into a small living room, he wondered what he could do to help his mate relax.

Beyond being honest with him, he wasn't sure. Would Gary even believe him if he told him he was here to give them a chance? It was clear he expected to be rejected. Chris wondered if a part of Gary thought that Chris would decide he wasn't worth it eventually, and that was why he was so willing to give him time to think things over.

Chris wouldn't reject his mate. He turned to Gary suddenly as they stopped by the couch. Gary's eyes widened when Chris cupped his cheek like he had over dinner the other day. Chris didn't give himself the chance to overthink what he was about to do and leaned forward to press their lips together as he wrapped an arm around Gary's waist.

Gary jerked back, probably not having expected that. Chris felt them fall, but there was nothing he could do. With his arm around Gary, they were linked together, so they went together. Chris tried to turn them around, but there wasn't enough space, and falling took only a second or two.

They landed on the couch, thankfully. He heard the breath whoosh out of Gary's lungs and tried to pull away, panicking at the thought he'd ruined everything. What had he been thinking, kissing Gary without asking him for permission first? He could have hurt both of them, and he wouldn't be surprised if Gary told him to fuck off.

But Gary didn't. He didn't even let Chris get to his feet. Instead, he wrapped his arms around Chris's neck, locking both of them into place.

Gary didn't want this to stop. He hadn't expected Chris to kiss him, which was the only excuse he had for having moved back and toppled both of them down.

Luckily, the couch was there. If they'd been anywhere else in the house, it would have hurt, but Gary had landed on a soft surface, and Chris was on top of him.

Gary was in heaven.

He hadn't known what to expect when he'd opened his door to find Chris standing there, and he still didn't. He wanted to ask Chris why he was here, why he'd kissed him, and what he'd do next, but at the same time, he was afraid that asking so many questions would send Chris running.

It probably wouldn't—Chris was here for a reason, and he'd been the one to initiate the kiss. That had to mean something, and Gary kept that in mind as he locked Chris into place with his arms.

Chris chuckled. "Sorry about that. I should have asked before kissing you."

Gary shook his head. "It's fine. You don't have to ask to kiss me because my answer will always be yes."

Chris pressed his elbows into the couch so his weight wouldn't all be on Gary. Gary couldn't say he minded either way as long as Chris wasn't going anywhere.

"I came here to talk, but I'm not sure where to start," Chris said.

"Maybe we don't need to talk right away."

Chris stared for a moment, and Gary expected him to reject his offer. Chris had said he was here to talk, and even though he'd kissed Gary, he might not want to repeat the experience. Gary was ready to apologize, but Chris leaned forward and kissed him again, and Gary decided that he probably didn't need to.

Gary tightened his hold on Chris and kissed him back. He couldn't remember the last time he'd done this, especially with someone he cared about. He hadn't been entirely celibate since he'd lost his clan, but he'd had other things to focus on, and for a long time, he hadn't thought he deserved anything like this, not even with someone who wasn't his mate. He still wasn't sure he did, but he wouldn't waste this opportunity. He had no idea if it meant that Chris accepted him or if he was just kissing him goodbye, but Gary wanted to enjoy the moment.

He wasn't sure how long they stayed on the couch, lazily making out as if they had all the time in the world. It felt oddly familiar, even though Gary was sure he'd never done this with anyone. Usually, when he was with someone, it was a means to an end. They both wanted pleasure, and the sooner they got it, the better. Kissing for what felt like hours on the couch had never happened, but he liked it, and he hoped he'd get to do it again.

Chris was the only person he wanted to do it with, though. Gary wasn't sure he could ever have anyone else if Chris rejected him. His heart hurt at the thought, but he'd accept Chris's decision if that was what Chris wanted. It wouldn't feel fair, but he wouldn't have a choice.

But it didn't feel like Chris was rejecting Gary. His weight on top of Gary was perfect, and he fit so well between Gary's legs and in his arms. Gary never wanted to let go, and kissing Chris made it easy to forget that there was a world outside of the living room.

Chris's lips were soft, but his kiss was demanding. He kissed like he knew what he wanted and wasn't afraid of demanding it, something Gary was jealous of. He knew what he wanted, but he was terrified at the thought of being honest about it. He could too easily imagine Chris deciding he wasn't worth it and leaving him behind. It might be the guilt talking, but it was a genuine possibility as far as he was concerned.

When Chris pushed away, Gary panicked. He tightened his hold around him, making him chuckle. Thankfully, Chris didn't seem offended. He also didn't stop moving though, and after a moment, Gary had to let him go.

Losing his mate's body on top of his made him feel like something was missing. He was tempted to beg Chris to come back, but he didn't. Instead, he quickly scrambled into a sitting position, settling next to Chris. He was afraid to look at his mate and of what he'd see if he did, but to his surprise, Chris took his hand and linked their fingers together. This didn't feel like a rejection. Gary supposed that anything was possible, but why would Chris come to him, make out with him on this couch, only to reject him?

"I didn't come here to make out," Chris began.

Gary's stomach churned. He shouldn't feel like a teenager

with his first crush, dammit. He was old enough to know better. He needed to be more in control and to stop assuming he knew what Chris was doing and what he wanted. He didn't have to freak out every time Chris did or said something he felt was a rejection. So far, none of them were.

Gary swallowed. "Why did you come, then?" He hoped Chris wasn't angry or feeling pressured. Considering Gary was smaller than him, he couldn't force him to do anything. He could manipulate him, but that wasn't the kind of person Gary was. He wanted Chris to be here of his own free will and to want to be with him as much as he wanted to be with Chris.

"I know we talked a lot over dinner, but that was mostly about the village and all of that," Chris said. "I want to know more about your past."

"I'll tell you everything you want to know, but there's not much. I had a happy life with my clan and my family until they were all killed." Gary shivered. "And that's not something I want to talk about."

Chris squeezed Gary's hand. "I won't ask you to talk about it. I can imagine how hard it was, and I have no reason to want you to relive that time. How about I tell you about my family?"

Gary was curious, so he nodded. He wanted to know more about Chris and his people. Chris had mentioned his best friend a few times, and Gary was curious about him.

"I didn't have an easy childhood. I wouldn't say my parents were abusive, but they were neglectful. I was left mostly to myself, and as an only child, I was lonely a lot of the time," Chris said.

He stroked the back of Gary's hand with his thumb. It didn't look like he was doing it on purpose. His gaze was lost as he talked about his past, and Gary wished he'd told his mate about his family now. It was clear Chris didn't want to talk about his, but he was.

"You don't have to tell me," Gary murmured.

"It's fine. Like I said, my parents weren't abusive. I didn't feel I had anyone until I met Ronnie, though. He's been my best friend since we were kids, and after we were attacked, he's the reason I decided to be a hunter. I was lucky. I survived the Kudlak attack without even a scratch, but the Kudlak really focused on Ronnie. He still has scars. He's been hiding in his apartment for a few years, never coming out. He has everything delivered to his doorstep and works from home. It was a slow decline, but he's a recluse."

"He's terrified."

Chris nodded. "I don't blame him. After what he's been through, I'd be surprised if he wasn't. I became a hunter because I wanted to show him that I could protect him, and that's still my goal. I never expected to find a family through the hunters. I want Ronnie to move here and be part of it, but I came to realize that even if he doesn't, I won't be alone. I have Boyd and Kendrick, Clay and the other hunters." Chris looked straight into Gary's eyes. "And I have you."

This wasn't what Chris had been planning to do. He *definitely* hadn't planned to kiss Gary, but thankfully, that part had gone well. Chris had wanted to continue kissing his mate for the rest of the day, but he'd remembered why he was there.

Gary was his mate, and he needed to be treated right. Kissing him was fine, but opening up to him and explaining why things might be tough for a while was better.

Chris knew that he had a hard time letting people in. He'd been neglected by the two people who should have made him the center of their universe, and it wasn't something he'd ever forget. He'd been lonely as a child, and while things had gotten better as he grew up, he didn't think he would ever forget it.

But he wasn't alone anymore, and like he'd told Gary, his mate was part of his new family. Chris wasn't saying it just because of the bond they shared. He truly believed it, and he wanted Gary to know.

Gary nodded. "You do have me."

"I freaked out when I found out about being your mate, and I'm sorry about that. There aren't many people in the world you feel have a duty toward you. There are your parents when you're a child, then the person you fall in love with or your mate. I know about the bond and what it means, so I guess I have certain expectations. I expect you not to leave me and to be there for me, but I expected my parents to do the same, and they never did."

"I can't make promises I might not be able to keep, but I can tell you that if it's in my power, I will never leave you."

They both knew they might not have a choice. Chris was a hunter. He regularly went out to fight Kudlaks. He'd seen a lot over the years, and Gary had seen just as much if not more. They knew what they were up against, but it wouldn't be enough for Chris to take a step back, and he didn't know how Gary would take that.

"I want to tell you the same," Chris said. "If I can avoid it, I won't leave you. I might not have any idea what I'm doing as a mate, but I feel this was a good start, and I want to get to know you." Chris grinned. "For example, is your name really Gary?"

Gary blinked. "I'm sorry?"

"It's not that I don't like it, but it doesn't really feel like a name a Vila would have."

"That's because it's a shortened version of my full name, Garretson."

That was a bit of a mouthful. "I see. Is your father's name Garrett, then?"

Gary grinned. "It was, yes. My mother insisted on naming

me, but he was always embarrassed. I think he was relieved when I started going by Gary."

There was sadness lurking in Gary's eyes, but it didn't seem like it would be enough to stop him. He might not want to share what had happened to his family and clan, but he had good memories of those people. He needed to cherish them.

It was a fine line to walk. Chris cherished the memories he had with Ronnie, but he couldn't cling to them because they were in the past. They could make new memories, but not with the distance between them. Chris couldn't go to Ronnie, which meant Ronnie would have to come to him.

Chris wasn't sure he ever would.

He cleared his throat. "My name is Chris, and it's not the shortened version of anything. Ronnie calls me Christopher when he's yelling at me, but it's not my name."

Gary snickered. "I think I'll like him if I ever meet him."

Chris wanted that so much it felt painful. He didn't have to choose between Gary and Ronnie because he already had, in a way. He'd told Ronnie he could never come back and that his place was in the village, and he'd meant it. His place *was* here, with Gary.

But he'd always miss Ronnie and the closeness they'd shared. If Ronnie ever moved here, Chris would have every-thing he could ever want from life. Even if his best friend stayed where he was, though, that didn't mean Chris would be alone. People weren't abandoning him. Gary certainly wasn't.

"I didn't expect to have a mate," Chris admitted. "And I'm not sure I'm ready for one. Honestly, even the thought of a serious relationship freaks me out right now. I've never had one beyond my friendships, and I don't know how to be-have."

"I think that's something we should decide together. I al-ready told you that I don't expect anything from you, and I wasn't lying. I understand how much of a shock this must have been, and you should take as much time as you need to wrap your mind around what's happening."

Chris wasn't sure he deserved a man like Gary. Gary gave so much more than Chris deserved, especially after the way Chris had treated him. Chris didn't feel he deserved it, but that didn't mean he was about to push Gary away.

"I'm thankful for all of that. No matter how freaked out I am, this feels right."

Gary smiled. "It does?"

"This is the perfect moment for me to meet my mate, isn't it? I'm settling down in the village and with the clan, and between that and everything else, I can see how wrong my life as a hunter was before. It's very different now, and while I'll always be afraid that I'll lose someone I care about, I know that if it happens, it won't be because they chose to leave me behind."

Chris knew this was a fear he developed as a child, and he needed to get over it. Gary wasn't abandoning him. Neither were Boyd and Kendrick or even Ronnie. Chris's parents had left him as soon as he turned eighteen, but that was almost twenty years ago, and it was time to let go of that pain. Chris's parents didn't deserve for him still to be hurt over what they'd done. They were assholes, and Chris didn't need them. His future was bright.

As long as he stopped being an idiot.

"I want to give our bond a chance," he told Gary. "I'm sure I'll mess things up and make mistakes, but I'm just as sure that we can deal with it together. I don't know much about the kind of paranormal being you are, so you'll have to tell me, but if the bond between us works like it does for shifters, then as long as we take things slow, I think I'll be all right."

Gary was visibly more relaxed now, and Chris had a hard time believing it was just because of his words. Gary had clearly been anxious about Chris accepting their bond, and Chris couldn't blame him. He'd run the first time they'd met, right after Gary told him they were mates. It hadn't been the best first impression, but Gary had continued giving Chris opportunities to show him he wouldn't continue running.

Chris wouldn't be like his parents. He wanted to make Gary happy, and that meant being there for him.

"It works a bit like for Nix," Gary explained. "We know from sight, but since we can shift into certain animals, we don't have the brand on our skin after we bond. We give the mating bite, like shifters."

This was news to Chris, and it made him realize he didn't know much about Gary. He knew Gary had lost everyone and his history, but not much about who Gary was, what he was, and what his hopes and dreams were. That was something he needed to fix.

But first, he needed Gary to know something. "I have a lot of questions, but I want you to be sure you want to give this a chance, too."

Gary appeared amused. "I wouldn't be here if I didn't."

"So you don't care that I'm a hunter? You don't care that I've killed countless of them over the years or that I intend to continue doing so?"

"They killed my family. I know that not all Kudlaks are bad, but it's hard to accept. I'm certain that none of the Kudlaks you killed were good people, though, so no. I don't care about that. I only care about you and the future we'll build together."

That was what Chris had wanted to hear.

Gary wasn't surprised by anything Chris was telling him. He wasn't a fighter, but after what had happened to his clan, he'd been tempted to hunt Kudlaks and destroy as many of them as he could find.

The problem was that the first Kudlak he'd stumbled onto had almost killed him. Gary hadn't meant to end up in that situation. He'd wanted Kudlaks to die, but he wasn't an idiot. That encounter had burned that into his memory, and while he'd never be a hunter, he understood why someone would want to be one and why it was necessary. Besides, it was what Krsniks had been created to do, and they and Vila had always had a somewhat symbiotic relationship.

They always shared villages and clans. Krsniks went out on hunts, killed Kudlaks, and protected the world. In exchange, the Vila kept the villages where the Krsnik clan lived safe. They took care of the wounded and made sure that the Krsniks could hunt without having to worry about what was happening at home. They taught them magic, and it wasn't unheard of for Krsniks and Vila to have relationships. Sometimes, they were even mates.

Gary understood all of that, and he understood watching people he cared about leaving the clan and possibly never coming back. It had happened too many times, and it might with Chris, too.

But Chris wasn't just a member of Gary's family. He was his mate, and Gary didn't know if he'd survive losing him. He couldn't even begin to imagine what it would feel like to have Chris leave home and never return.

He didn't want to think about it right now, and he certainly didn't want to imagine it. He didn't know what would happen between him and Chris, but he could tell that Chris was honest when he said that he wanted to give their bond a chance. Gary wanted the same. He couldn't allow fear to stop him. It wouldn't be fair to Chris or to himself.

But Chris needed to know about what had happened to Gary so he would understand why Gary might freak out every time he went on a hunt. It might not help, but just like

Chris had told Gary about his past and what had happened with Ronnie, it was something they had to share.

"I want to tell you what happened to my clan," Gary said.

"You don't have to. I want to know because it happened to you, but it's not necessary to tell me now, or ever if you never feel up to it."

Gary smiled. "And that's why I want to tell you."

"If you do, I'll listen."

Gary closed his eyes because it would be easier. "Like always, the Krsniks all had a hunt to go on. At that time, we were in the middle of a war with other clans, so they headed out every day. They were tired, and we all knew something was going to break eventually. We kept losing people, and there weren't enough of us to continue protecting the village the way it should have been protected. Our hunters were out when we were attacked. I had never seen so many Kudlaks work together, and I hope I never see it again. There was one especially who kept cackling and saying he was going to finish his set, no matter what happened."

Gary remembered that, because it had been so odd that it had pierced through his fear and panic. He hadn't had a lot of time to focus on that Kudlak, though.

"They managed to breach the ward," he continued. "We were strong, but the Kudlaks were stronger. No one knew what to do. The people left in the village weren't fighters, but we did our best. I was wounded, but it was nothing next to what the others went through. I lost everyone that day. I had to make a choice, as the village was on fire, and I did the only thing I could. I was in pain and terrified, and I hid."

Gary swallowed and looked down at his hand. His fingers were still linked with Chris's, and he half expected his mate to pull away and tell him that he'd been a coward. He'd told himself that every day since the clan had been attacked, and he believed it.

But he also believed that if he'd fought harder, he'd be dead right now, and he wouldn't have met his mate. Chris would have been fine since he was human, but Gary didn't want to imagine him with anyone else. He was Gary's.

"I can tell you blame yourself for hiding," Chris said gently. "I understand why. I hope you know that you had no other choice. You would have died if you'd stood up to the Kudlaks."

Gary's eyes filled with tears. He didn't want to shed them, so he looked up, hoping it would be enough to stop him from crying. He was making himself vulnerable, and he didn't need to make it worse.

"Logically, I know you're right," he admitted. "Nothing I could have done on my own would have saved the clan. Emotionally, it feels like I failed them, and I'm afraid I'll do the same to you. There's also the fact that there's a chance that one day you won't come back from a fight, and that's hard to wrap my mind around. I already lost so many people. I don't want to lose you, too."

Chris wrapped an arm around Gary's shoulders and pulled him close. He kissed the top of Gary's head, and Gary allowed himself to take comfort in his mate's presence. It was the first time he'd had someone to comfort him like this. Even if he had, it wouldn't have been the same.

Gary only had one mate, and he was in his arms right now. He still didn't understand what he'd done to deserve this happiness, but he told himself that he didn't need to have done anything. He'd suffered enough. He'd watched his entire family and every person he cared about die. Maybe that was enough for Fate to want him to be happy.

As long as she didn't snatch Chris away from Gary anytime soon, Gary thought he would be fine. He couldn't even think about losing his mate, but he told himself he didn't have to. Chris was young and strong. He never went on hunting trips alone. He did everything he could to win his fights and come home.

Gary straightened, even though he wanted to stay in Chris's embrace. "I talked to Alexis, and he said he can help me train. I want to be able to defend myself and others."

Chris frowned. "Are you sure that's advisable? I'm not saying you shouldn't do this if you want to, but unless you have years of training, you probably won't win against a Kudlak. That's why humans don't hunt them alone. It's better in twos or threes. That's how Kendrick, Boyd, and I became friends. We were stuck together a lot of the time, and we learned to trust each other with our lives."

"I don't expect to ever be able to defeat a Kudlak on my own, but I don't need to. As long as I can defend myself and anyone around me long enough that better-trained people can arrive, I'll be fine."

Chris didn't look convinced, but he didn't try to change Gary's mind. That was good, because Gary was pretty sure he'd give his mate anything he asked for, no matter how he felt about it. He realized it was stupid and that the only reason he felt like that was that he was afraid to lose Chris.

But he wouldn't. He wouldn't allow anyone to take his mate away, be it himself or the circumstances. Whatever happened next, he and Chris would face it together.

"I don't know about you, but I feel a bit lighter," Chris said as he pulled Gary toward him again.

"I do. I never like talking about what happened, but it was the right thing to do today."

Chris's smile was gentle. "We both need to learn to let go of the guilt."

"Maybe we can learn together."

Chris's eyes sparkled as he leaned forward to kiss Gary. Gary didn't know what the future held and if he'd ever be able to get over how he felt about his lost clan, but he would try. He owed it to himself and to Chris to heal and be ready if anything happened again.

CHAPTER FOUR

"Where do you think we should put them?" Dermot asked.

Tamlin looked out at the area around the village. Gary knew what he was doing. He wanted to include as much of the village as possible in the magical wards, but at the same time, there weren't enough of them to make the wards sturdy enough. The bigger the wards, the weaker they would be. They might even be vulnerable enough to be broken.

Like they had been when Gary's village had been attacked.

Gary swallowed and looked at the dry earth he was standing on. The ward had been strong, but not strong enough. He still didn't know what had happened or how the Kudlaks had managed to get in, and sometimes, he wondered if it mattered. Knowing wouldn't bring back the people he loved, and it wouldn't change the fact that they were dead. At the same time, though, knowing more might help him find peace.

Tamlin sighed. "I don't think we should go beyond the last houses."

Dermot grimaced. "I'd hoped you'd have better news."

"We can't go bigger. Maybe once more people start arriving, but not right now. It would be too taxing on us, and even if we tried, I don't think they'd be strong enough."

Dermot nodded and looked in the distance. Gary did the same. Every one of them wanted to protect the village. This was their new home, and after what they'd lived through, they wanted to feel safe here. Gary wasn't sure he ever would, and it had nothing to do with the new clan or the people who belonged to it. He'd been supposedly safe with his old clan, too. Instead, they'd ended up in a war with other clans, and the Kudlaks had exterminated the people left behind.

This time around, it wasn't looking great, either, and Gary wondered if he was setting himself up for heartache or death. He'd already decided that if they were attacked, he wouldn't run, but even though he'd started training with Alexis, he still didn't have a clue what he was doing in a fight. That was why the village needed better wards, which in turn was why he and the others were here, discussing how to make them. They had no idea how long they'd have to sustain these wards before they could change to better ones, and there was no way for them to find out. The news that a new clan had been created was spreading, and more people arrived every week, but it was still only a trickle and not enough for the village to be safe.

"Maybe we could contact other people," Anita suggested. "I mean, we all know Vila we crossed paths with when we were on the run, right? I don't know about you, but I have a few phone numbers of people who could be interested in moving here. I didn't want to say anything because I wasn't sure they'd be welcome, but now that we've lived with the clan for a little while, I know they would be. We need them, and I think they might need the clan."

Gary frowned. Why had he not thought of that? He was safe now, but some of the people he'd met when he'd been on the run probably weren't. He should have thought to call them and offer them a spot with the clan, but he'd been too focused on his own safety and living his life. Did that make him selfish? Maybe, but he was still in time to change that.

Dermot and Tamlin looked at each other.

Gary couldn't read their expressions, but he thought they were all on the same page. They needed more people.

"I think it's a good idea," Tamlin said. "We need to

convince everyone we can think of to move here. It's the only way to keep the village safe, and I don't know about you, but I'm done running. Even if something happens to the clan, I'm not leaving. Not again."

Dermot grinned. "We should highlight that people find their mates when they move here."

The three of them turned as one toward Gary, who rolled his eyes. "And what if they don't find their mate when they get here?"

Dermot shrugged. "They might not, but they also might. I mean, you found your mate in the village. Alexis did, too. It's worth mentioning, at the very least. It means that even if people are somewhat safe wherever they are, they might want to come around and see if their mate is a clan member."

It had just been Gary and Alexis until now, but it was a big coincidence. Maybe Dermot wasn't wrong. They were building a new village where people would be safe and able to build a life. As they settled down, more of them would meet their mates or enter relationships. Besides, if it meant that more people would move, it would be worth mentioning.

Anita bumped her shoulder against Gary's. "How are things going with him?"

There was no reason for Gary to blush, but he felt his face heat. He didn't like being at the center of attention, and right now his three friends were staring at him. They looked hungry for news, which Gary could understand. He was sure they were hoping they'd meet their mate, too. Didn't everyone? Now that they were safe and had a home, it was time for them to put down roots, and what better way to do so than having a mate? Gary was one of the lucky ones, and everyone hoped they would be, too.

He smiled, unable to stop himself. "Things have been a little shaky, but we're working it out."

Anita beamed while Dermot slapped Gary's shoulder.

"How did he take it? He's human, right?"

"He is, which means there will be a little adjusting, but not that much. We had a talk, and we were honest with each other, which has made things smoother. I don't think he's ready to bond yet, but I'm not in a rush."

"He's fragile," Tamlin pointed out. "I don't know about you, but I'm not used to living with humans. It's odd to watch them around the village and think they can stand up to Kudlaks."

"Tamlin!" Dermot scolded.

"What? I'm right. I don't want Gary to worry, but his mate isn't a Krsnik. Something might happen when he's out on a hunt, which is why I thought Gary would want to bond with him as soon as possible."

Gary's happiness had only lasted a few moments. He didn't need Tamlin to tell him how precarious the situation was.

Did he want to bond with Chris? Of course he did. There was nothing he wanted more. But Chris wasn't ready, and Gary would honor that. It wouldn't be fair to force Chris into a situation he wasn't ready for just because Gary was afraid.

The sound of someone running made all of them jump and turn. The person wasn't running toward them but rather toward the edge of the village, and they weren't alone. Gary noticed several others following, all of them wearing their hunter gear.

He swallowed and took his phone out. He hadn't realized he'd had a text from Chris, and he quickly opened it. His stomach dropped as soon as he saw the words on his screen. "They found a nest."

Dermot swore and squeezed Gary's shoulder. "He'll be fine. He's not going out there alone, and I'm sure both Clay and Rowan will be with them."

"I hate that they nest now," Anita muttered.

Gary did, too. Things had been hard enough when Krsniks had been hunting lone Kudlaks. Now, they had to deal with couples and sometimes nests. Gary could only imagine what they found in those nests. It made his stomach churn.

That was where his mate was going. He might not be going alone, but he'd still be surrounded by Kudlaks and vulnerable. Gary wanted to scream, but instead, he pressed his lips together.

Chris was a hunter. Gary understood better why he'd chosen that life after Chris had told him about his best friend, but that didn't mean he wasn't terrified.

What if Chris didn't come home today?

"Why are you here again?" Kendrick teased. His smile was at odds with the way they all felt.

Boyd grimaced. "I couldn't stay at home knowing that both of you and Alexis are headed out. I want to know what's going on."

Chris understood. He wasn't sure he'd continue hunting if he felt he had a choice. He'd started doing so to get revenge, but mostly, it had been to make the world a better place and to ensure that Ronnie would feel safe. He still hadn't achieved that. There were still plenty of Kudlaks and other monsters, and worse, they were starting to organize and hunt in families—if that was what you could call them. The world still wasn't a safe place, and while Chris realized it probably never would be, he'd do what he could to make it happen.

"Have you called Gary?" Boyd asked.

Chris shook his head. "I texted him, but I didn't stop to call him." Chris wasn't sure he could stand it if Gary asked him to stay at the village.

They'd all gotten a group text telling them a Kudlak nest had been found and that they'd be heading out soon. They'd been told to meet at Clay and Rowan's house to get more information, which was different from how Cornelius used to do things. He hadn't cared how many hunters he lost when they went out. Even when they found nests, he just told people to go to a certain address and threw them off the deep end. Those who survived were strong, and those who died, well, they should have been stronger.

Chris shuddered. He was ever so thankful to be rid of Cornelius. The man should never have been the leader of anything, let alone people who put their lives in danger every day. He couldn't help but wonder how the other hunters were doing, but it didn't matter. They'd made their choice, just like Chris, Boyd, and Kendrick.

When they reached the house, several people were standing in front. Rowan and Clay were on the porch, talking. Their expressions were grim, which told Chris everything he needed to know.

He swallowed. This was the first time he was heading out on a hunt since meeting Gary, and he wasn't sure how it would change things. He was sure it would, and he felt more nervous because he knew Gary would be waiting for him, but did it mean he wouldn't be able to focus? He sure hoped not. Not being able to focus could mean death when he was fighting Kudlaks, and he wasn't willing to risk that.

It was odd. Even before, Chris had Ronnie and the other hunters. He'd always had someone waiting for him when he returned from hunts, but not in the same way. He could imagine all too well how Gary would feel when he saw his text, and he wished he could make things easier on his mate. The only way to do that would be to stop going on hunts, though, and that wasn't something Chris was willing to consider at the moment.

Luckily, he didn't have time to obsess over it and tie himself in knots. More people were arriving, and Clay gestured at them to follow as he hopped off his porch. Rowan was behind him, looking like the lethal Krsnik he was. Sometimes Chris felt inadequate because he was only human, but even though it took at least two or three of them to kill a Kudlak, that didn't make him weak. Sure, they were weaker and not as fast, but they trained for this, and they knew what they were doing. Even more than before, they were protected. They now had several Krsniks working with them, keeping them safe as they took down the Kudlaks. Things had gotten better.

Chris prayed they wouldn't get worse.

He and the others followed their leaders to the edge of the village. Chris knew the wards were in place, but they weren't very strong. There were also devices to block anyone from shimmering into the village, which was why they were meeting the Nix, who would shimmer them in and out at the edge of it.

The pink-haired nuisance wasn't there today. These two Nix were blond, and their expressions were serious. They were wearing uniforms, and when Chris got close enough, he recognized them as enforcers. Maybe they'd stick around to help fight. Even if they didn't, they knew what they were doing more than Nysys. Hopefully, they'd talk less.

Rowan turned toward their group. There weren't as many of them as Chris wished, and without Boyd, he and Kendrick would have to learn to fight without him. It made Chris nervous, but he knew staying back made Boyd happy, and that was what he wanted for his friend.

All of them had lost someone or had been hurt. Chris was the exception, although he felt that, in some ways, he'd lost Ronnie, even though he was still alive. Boyd had lost his sister to a Kudlak, which was why he'd become a hunter. He'd made his peace with her death, and he wouldn't be coming on hunts anymore. Chris was sure Alexis was relieved.

"We don't have a lot of information," Rowan warned. "This town contacted the council. They've had people vanishing for a few weeks now, and they found some of them dead, all their blood gone. From the many disappearances, there's no way this is a lone Kudlak. That means we're looking at least at a couple, but with the number of people involved, I'm betting there are more of them."

Kendrick groaned. "I hate it when they nest."

Chris shared that feeling. It wasn't only because it was more dangerous for them, but also because the nests tended to be nasty. Kudlaks dragged their victims into their nests, played with them for as long as they could, then drank them dry and discarded their bodies. He was surprised that some of the bodies had been found. It wasn't unheard of for Kudlaks to leave them to decay in their nests until they were ready to move on.

"You know what to do. I have a good idea of where the nest is located, so we'll shimmer there. Alexis, I want you with Chris and Kendrick."

Alexis nodded. He stood nearby, leaning against Boyd, who had an arm around his shoulders. They were both tense, and while in a way Chris wished Gary were here the way Boyd was for Alexis, he was also glad he hadn't come. Chris wouldn't have known how to behave. He and Gary weren't close enough that they could bid each other goodbye like that.

Alexis's friend, Caroline, stood with Rachel. They seemed to have decided to work together, which made them a lethal pair. Rachel had always been strong, and more than that, she was a skilled fighter. She never hesitated to kick Chris's ass when they trained, and Chris was glad for that. He knew that if he could take on Rachel, he could take on a pissed-off Kudlak.

Caroline was a Krsnik. She was wearing hunter gear—all in black—and she was clearly comfortable in it. She'd arrived with Alexis, and Chris knew that the two of them had been hunting Kudlaks all their lives. They hadn't had clans to protect anymore, but they'd banded with another friend and made a little family. They'd been integrated into the village, and now they had an even bigger family to protect. Caroline looked like she wouldn't hesitate to tear off heads if it struck her fancy.

The Kudlaks wouldn't know what hit them.

A movement outside of the wards made Chris turn. He groaned at the sight of pink hair. Sometimes he wondered why Nysys had decided that he needed to come with them every time they found a nest. He didn't think the Nix had a death wish. Likely he was bored. Chris wished Nysys would find something else to do if that was the case.

Gary tried to focus on the wards and the conversation between his friends, but he couldn't. How was he supposed to when his mate was leaving the safety of the village to attack a Kudlak nest? The only thing Gary could think of was what would happen if Chris was hurt or, worse, killed. No matter how many times he told himself that Chris was a good fighter and wouldn't be facing the Kudlaks alone, his brain would show him images he'd rather not see.

It wasn't just Chris. Other people Gary cared about were going on that hunt, like Alexis. Of course, Alexis was a Krsnik, so his chances of coming home in one piece were higher. Hopefully, since he was friends with Gary, he'd keep an eye on Chris and ensure he returned home safely.

Gary couldn't imagine how Clay and Rowan did it. Maybe it was easier when both of them were out on hunts, but he couldn't imagine it would be. At least at home, Gary couldn't see how bad things were. Clay and Rowan would both be there, and while they'd protect each other, they would be in the front row to watch if something happened to the other.

"You should probably go home," Dermot said gently.

It took Gary a moment to realize he was talking to him. "I'm sorry. I swear I'm listening."

Tamlin shook his head. "I have no doubt that you are, but Dermot is right. You won't be able to focus, and none of us expect you to. Right now, your mate is your only focus, which is as it should be. Go home and wait for Chris. We can meet again to talk about the wards tomorrow or in a few days. The wards that are currently active are good enough for a while."

Gary bit his lower lip. He wanted to help the village, but he wasn't sure he'd be able to think about anything that wasn't Chris until Chris returned. That wouldn't help Dermot, Tamlin, and Anita. They needed him to be attentive to what he was doing so he wouldn't make mistakes while pulling up new wards. Gary had to do the best he could to keep the village safe, and he wouldn't be if he was focused on Chris.

He sighed. "Fine. I'll head out, but call me if you decide anything."

"We won't decide today," Tamlin said. "Besides, we have to start calling the people we met over the years to convince them to visit. I think it would be best to wait until we know if people are coming before we touch the wards. If we manage to convince even two or three people, we can use their magic to make the wards stronger."

Gary was glad to leave. If he was going to freak out — and he had no doubt he would — he wanted to do so in private. This would be his life from now on, and he needed to learn to deal with it. Unfortunately, he had no idea how. He was anxious and angry at himself for not being able to help the hunters, and at the same time, he was angry because Chris was doing the right thing. Gary wanted nothing more than to tell him he had to stop being a hunter, but he could tell that wouldn't go down well. Besides, it was his fear talking.

Would he rather have Chris stay home? Yes. He'd be happy if he never had to worry about his mate ever again. Chris might even consider the idea if Gary brought it up, but he wouldn't, or at least, he didn't think he would. He didn't actually want Chris to stop being a hunter, because that wasn't what Chris wanted. They might be mates, but they both had their own dreams and things they felt they needed to do. This was Chris's, no matter how anxious it made Gary.

Gary didn't want to leave the village and the clan, but this reminded him too much of when he'd lost his clan. The hunters were all going out, leaving the village behind, unprotected beyond the wards.

Gary sucked in a breath and looked in the distance. From where he was, he couldn't see Whitedell or the house where the pride lived, but they were close enough that the pride could be here in seconds if anything happened. Gary had to remember that.

His clan had been decimated during a very different time. The clans had been at war back then, which meant no one had come to help. His new clan had friends. The Whitedell pride would be here to save them if they ever needed it, and while they couldn't do anything about Chris, knowing that the village was safe enough helped Gary relax. Not a lot, but he didn't feel like screaming as he walked home.

Before he got there, he noticed Devon sitting on the porch of the house Clay and Rowan lived in. Devon was a human teenager, and to everyone's surprise, he'd been found with two Kudlaks. Gary hadn't known what to think of them when he'd first heard about it. He'd been sure the Kudlak kept Devon with her so she could feed her daughter and herself, but from what Gary now knew, they'd never hurt Devon. As far as he could tell, there wasn't even a single bite mark on Devon's body, even though he'd lived with the Kudlaks for a while.

Why was he waiting in front of Clay and Rowan's house? Gary was curious. Maybe talking to Devon would help distract him.

Instead of walking toward home, he headed toward the boy. Devon looked up with wide eyes when he heard Gary, but his shoulders slumped when he saw who it was.

"I'm sorry I'm a disappointment," Gary teased.

Devon's cheeks flushed. "It's fine. I'm just nervous because they all went out."

Gary nodded and gestured at the steps on which Devon was sitting. "May I?"

"This isn't my house. You can do whatever you want."

"I don't want to bother you if you're not up for company, but I wouldn't mind talking to someone."

Devon stared at Gary for a moment before nodding. "Your mate went out on the hunt."

Gary shouldn't be surprised that Devon knew Chris was his mate. The village was tiny, and he was pretty sure that every person who lived here knew about him and Chris. That was how things went when so many people lived close to each other.

He sat down, careful to keep some distance between them. He didn't know how the boy would react to his presence.

Devon stared for a moment. "You're not a Krsnik."

Gary shook his head. "I'm a Vila."

"Melissa told me about them."

"Is Melissa your mother?"

"No. My mother kicked me out. Melissa is the woman who took me in and protected me." Devon hesitated. "She's a Kudlak."

Gary nodded. "I know."

"You don't care about it?"

"As long as she doesn't hurt the people I love, I don't. I've seen too much to believe that all Kudlaks are bad people or that all Krsniks are good."

"She's a good person. She protected me, and she never once hurt me. Her daughter didn't, either."

"Then I'm glad you found them. Why did your parents kick you out? You're so young."

"I just turned eighteen." His cheeks flushed, and he looked away. "They found me kissing the neighbor."

Gary frowned. "I don't understand."

"He was a boy. They didn't want me kissing boys, and they kicked me out. I think they believed that I'd come back to them and promise to do what they wanted, but I couldn't. I can't erase part of myself just because they don't like it." He snapped his mouth shut.

He probably felt he'd said too much, but Gary didn't mind. "I'm sorry they did that to you. They shouldn't have."

Devon shrugged. "It's fine. I got used to it, and if they hadn't kicked me out, I wouldn't be here today."

Gary supposed he was right. If his clan hadn't been decimated, he wouldn't be here today, either. He wouldn't have met his mate.

Gary would always mourn the people he'd lost, and he suspected he'd always feel guilty about not being able to do anything to help them, but he wouldn't have been able to change anything even if he'd tried harder. He hadn't been the one to hurt his people. The Kudlaks had done that, and he had no fault in what had happened.

If only he could fully believe it.

Chris punched the Kudlak in the nose. Normally it wouldn't do much damage, but the Kudlak was already wounded, and she reeled back, her face a mask of blood. Chris grinned at the sound of the satisfying crunch and at the wail she let out. He always felt good when he fought Kudlaks, but this time was even better.

These Kudlaks had been kidnapping people from the nearby towns since they'd arrived in the area, terrorizing them and draining them dry before abandoning their bodies where they fell. The place stank to high heaven and was a mess of blood and decomposing bodies that had made Chris's stomach churn when he'd first stepped inside. From what he'd seen, he was pretty sure the Kudlaks had been torturing these poor people, and he wanted revenge for them. It might not be his place, but he didn't care.

Kendrick was fighting next to him. When the Kudlak stepped back after Chris's punch, he lunged forward. He had two knives in his hands, and he sank both of them into the woman's chest. She screeched, and for a moment, it was as if time stopped. Chris stared at her as she realized what had happened and that she was about to die. She made a move toward Kendrick, no doubt to push him away, but it was too late. He had his knives in her, and he knew how to use them.

Chris watched as Kendrick twisted the blades, then dragged them through the Kudlak's chest. Blood gushed as her body slumped, and Kendrick quickly stepped back.

Something heavy hit Chris, sending him slamming against the wall. Pain burned in his shoulder, and he yelped, quickly turning around to see what was happening. There was a knife stuck in his shoulder. He stared at it, wondering how it had gotten there.

He wasn't sure he could continue fighting. He knew it would be stupid to take it out, because it would start the blood flow, but at the same time, if he took it out, he might be able to continue kicking ass.

The Kudlak who'd stabbed him was coming toward him. The man looked feral, and a shiver of fear slid down Chris's spine. He had to remember that he wasn't alone. Even if he couldn't fight anymore, no one would allow the Kudlak to kill him.

But Kendrick and Alexis were both busy, so Chris turned to face the Kudlak. He raised his sword, trying to ignore the pain that flashed down his body. The Kudlak cackled. He sounded unhinged, which wasn't a surprise, considering the state of the place they'd nested in.

The Kudlaks had nested in an abandoned cabin at the edge of town. Chris wasn't sure how they'd found it, but from the state of it, it had been empty for a while. Luckily, it was only one room, so when he and the other hunters had barged in, they'd only had to worry about the Kudlaks they could see, but the nest was bigger than they'd expected. They'd thought they'd have to fight two or three Kudlaks, but there had been seven of them, and some were still standing.

"Oh no, you don't," a voice Chris didn't expect said.

Boyd appeared, raising two knives. He placed himself between Chris and the Kudlak, and from his stance, it was clear he was ready to fight.

Chris didn't want him to. Boyd didn't want to fight and continue killing Kudlaks, and everyone respected that. Why was he even here?

"Where the fuck did you come from?" Chris asked.

Boyd quickly turned to wink at Chris. "You're not happy to see me?"

"I'm delighted to see you, but I didn't think you'd be here." He was supposed to stay behind now that he'd decided to retire from the hunters. He hadn't been with Chris when they'd been shimmered here, but Chris should have noticed him sooner.

Movement beyond Boyd made Chris straighten, but he relaxed when he saw that Kendrick and Alexis had turned their attention to the Kudlak who'd stabbed him. Boyd wouldn't have to step in.

Boyd seemed to realize the same thing and quickly moved to Chris. "I was too anxious. When you shimmered away, I decided I needed to come along. I stayed on the edge of the fights, and I'm glad I'm here because it means I can help you. Come on. Let's find one of the Nix so you can go home."

Chris shook his head. "I'm not going anywhere until the fight is over."

Boyd rolled his eyes. "Of course you're not. It would be too much to expect you to be reasonable."

He wasn't wrong, but Chris wouldn't abandon his friends. Luckily, Boyd seemed to understand that. He stood by Chris's side, facing the fight, protecting him even though Chris didn't need it. He might be wounded, but it was nothing he hadn't gone through before.

He ignored the ache in his shoulder and kept his focus on the fights happening around him. Luckily, everything seemed to be under control. There had been seven Kudlaks, but there were plenty of hunters to fight them. Kendrick and Alexis worked together. Rachel and Caroline and Clay and Rowan did the same. The other hunters were paired off or in threes, and with three Kudlaks already on the ground, Boyd and Chris wouldn't have to worry for long.

Chris leaned against the nearest wall and winced. He really could have done without getting stabbed, dammit. It would take him out of the next few raids unless he managed to convince Rowan and Clay he was all right. Thankfully, he had several Nix he could ask to heal him. The two who'd shimmered him and the others here were fighting, too. Nysys wasn't, but then he never did. He usually hung out at the edge of the fight, watching and cheering the hunters on.

It was fucking weird.

As soon as the last Kudlak hit the ground, Boyd waved at Nysys. The man's expression turned to worry when he saw the knife sticking out of Chris's shoulder, and he hurried over.

"You could have told me earlier. I would have taken you back to the village right away."

Boyd arched a brow at Chris, but Chris ignored him. "I didn't want to go until I was sure we'd won the fight."

Nysys rolled his eyes. "You're trying to be the strong guy, huh? I don't understand why you guys always do that. What's wrong with being hurt and in pain? I mean, no one wants to feel that, but you do have a knife sticking from your shoulder."

"I'm fine," Chris said through gritted teeth.

"Sure you are. Everyone would be fine with that thing there, right?"

The guy was always annoying, but right now, he was extremely so. Chris wanted nothing more than to go home, have someone take the knife out, and heal him.

He sighed. Nysys was a Nix. "Can you heal me?"

"Nope."

Chris blinked. "What? Why not? You're a Nix."

"I am, but I'm not a healer. I can heal wounds, but not a freaking knife in the back. I wouldn't even know where to start taking it out."

"You wrap your fingers around it and pull until it's free."

"That sounds nasty, and I'm tempted to do it just to torture you a bit, but my answer is still no. What if I make it worse?" He grabbed Chris's good arm. "I'll take you home so someone else can take care of you."

They were gone before Chris could tell him he wanted to talk to Clay and Rowan first. Thankfully, Boyd was still there, so he'd be able to tell them what had happened to Chris and that he'd been Nysys-napped.

They appeared at the edge of the village by Rowan and Clay's house. Chris wasn't surprised to see several people had gathered there, no doubt eager to find out how the fight had gone. Devon was there, probably waiting for Kendrick since he had a massive crush on him. A few other people were present, but Chris's gaze snagged on Gary, who was talking to one of the men he'd arrived at the village with.

"We need a medic!" Nysys yelled dramatically.

Chris glared at him, but it was too late. The damage had already been done. Several people gasped, and Gary went pasty white when he saw Chris standing next to Nysys.

"Was that really necessary?" Chris asked.

Nysys grinned. "I always wanted to say that. Besides, you strike me as the kind of guy who's going to hide that you're hurt if you can get away with it. This way, you won't be able to."

He wasn't wrong. Chris had been planning to hide his wound until it was healed. He hadn't planned to tell Gary about it, but he should have known better.

Gary reached them quickly. He was still pale, but the fact that Chris was on his feet and talking probably helped him not freak out. He frowned when he saw the knife sticking out of Chris's back, then took his hand and pulled him forward.

"I need to find someone to help me," Chris said.

"I will." Gary's voice was uncompromising. "And I won't take no for an answer. You're coming home with me, and you'll stay there until you're healed."

"It would be faster if we found a Nix."

Gary abruptly stopped and turned to scowl at Chris. "I don't care how fast you want your wound healed. I'll be the one to take care of you, and I'll decide how much rest you need. And you *will* rest."

Chris could see he wouldn't win this fight, so he nodded and allowed his mate to drag him forward.

He hadn't expected this reaction when Gary had told him they were mates, but he should have. It made sense that Gary wanted to take care of him and ensure he was healthy and healed correctly.

Chris had no idea how to deal with it, but he supposed that going along with Gary's orders was a good start.

CHAPTER FIVE

Things had been tense, to say the least. Gary hated it, but even more he hated how terrified he'd been when he'd realized Chris had been hurt. He wasn't willing to play with his mate's health, which was why he was keeping an eye on Chris, even though he'd relented and had asked Nysys to heal him after checking for himself that the wound wasn't deep enough to create problems.

He frowned. He knew Nix healing was good, and he'd seen the wound for himself, but part of him didn't trust the Nix. What if he'd only healed the wound superficially? What if, under Chris's skin, there was still a wound that might get infected?

He couldn't stop thinking about that as he put together a breakfast tray and brought it to Chris. He'd been staying with Gary since he'd been hurt, and while Gary knew it was overkill, he didn't care about that, either. He wasn't going to lose his mate, dammit. He'd keep an eye on him until he was sure the wound had been healed completely.

He knocked on the guest room door. He'd been tempted to have Chris stay in his bedroom, but things had been awkward between them, and it felt like a good idea to give both of them space. It wasn't what Gary wanted, but it was what was best for both of them at the moment.

Gary could admit, at least to himself, that he was angry. He wished Chris would stop being a hunter and putting himself in danger, but he knew that even if he brought the idea up, Chris would dismiss it. He didn't want to stop being a hunter.

He wanted to continue hunting Kudlaks and keep the world safe, and while Gary understood that drive, he wasn't sure he could live with it.

He wasn't giving up on his mate, but something had to break, and he didn't know if it would be him or Chris. Probably him.

"Yes?" Chris called out.

Gary pushed open the door, only to stop moving when he saw that Chris was on the floor, doing push-ups. Gary's heart raced, and he quickly put down the tray. "You shouldn't be doing that. You're wounded." He fretted as he gestured for Chris to get to his feet.

His mate was only wearing a tank top, so Gary could see part of the scar the wound had left behind. The sight made his mouth go dry, and when Chris didn't get up as quickly as Gary wanted, he frowned and gestured at him again.

Chris sighed and obeyed. His hair was messy, and there was a light shine of sweat on his face, a sure indication that the push-ups weren't the first exercise he was doing.

Chris flopped onto the bed and stared at Gary. "I'm not wounded anymore, Gary."

"You can't know that. The wound is healed on the outside, but you don't know what's happening on the inside." Gary turned back toward the tray. He needed something to do with his hands.

"I'd feel it if it weren't healed. I'm completely fine. There's no pain. It doesn't even ache."

Gary understood he was being ridiculous. It was a miracle that Chris was still here instead of having told him to fuck off and left right after Nysys healed him. Gary was overbearing, and right now, he was also unreasonable.

He didn't have a say in what Chris did or didn't do, just like he didn't have a say in the fact that Chris would continue being a hunter. Part of him wanted to throw a tantrum because Chris was his mate, which meant he *should* have a say in it, but he reminded himself that Chris was an adult and his own man. He didn't need to ask Gary for permission to do things like push-ups, and he'd been a hunter long before the two of them met. It wasn't fair to request he stop hunting Kudlaks, and Gary knew it, which was why he hadn't.

Even though every time he thought about it, his heart broke a little more.

Gary carried the tray to the bed. He didn't look Chris in the eyes because he was afraid of what he'd see there, so while he waited for Chris to settle into a comfortable position, he stared at his mate's pillow. He'd been grateful that the guest room was clean and furnished when he'd decided to move Chris into his house, but part of him wished it hadn't been so that Chris would have had to stay with him.

It was ridiculous. They could have gone to Chris's house, or Chris could just have gone home, because he'd been fine after Nysys had healed him. He didn't need to stay with Gary. He didn't need Gary to keep an eye on him. Gary was overthinking everything, and he was pretty sure everyone knew it.

Including Chris.

"You don't have to do any of this," Chris murmured when he took the tray Gary offered.

"Any of what? Taking care of you? Making sure you have food or that your wound is healed?"

"Yes. My wound is healed. I was fine right after Nysys took care of me. I realize you don't know him and that he's a lot, but that doesn't mean his healing ability isn't good. You *know* I'm fine. You've been watching me since I returned from the raid."

Gary wasn't sure what to say, so he was grateful when Chris's phone vibrated on the nightstand. That only lasted for a moment. Seconds later, as he watched Chris reach for it, he realized that it could be a call to go on another raid.

He watched Chris's expression to try to understand who it was. He wasn't surprised to see Chris turn grim, and when Chris put the tray on the bed to get up, Gary knew he'd run out of time.

"What happened?" he asked.

Chris grabbed his socks from the dresser and sat back on the bed to put them on. "That was a group text from Clay. There's another nest."

"He can't be asking you to go. You're barely healed."

"He's not asking me in particular to go, but I'm fine. I'm not going to let the others go on their own when I'm as good as new."

"You were wounded just a few days ago. You need more rest and to sit this one out."

What would happen if Chris went? He might be healed, but his arm was probably still weak from the wound, and it could give him problems at the worst of times. Knowing Kudlaks, they would take advantage of that. Gary couldn't allow that to happen. Chris had to realize how bad things were and tell Clay that he couldn't come today.

"I'm not going to sit this one out," Chris snapped. He pressed his lips together, then looked up at Gary as he grabbed his shoes from under the bed. "I'm perfectly fine. I promise you that I feel no pain and that I wouldn't be going if I did."

"You're a hunter. Of course you'd go even if you were in pain." Gary sounded bitter because he was. He hated all of this. He'd thought he could accept that Chris was a hunter, but he wasn't sure he could anymore.

Chris put on his boots, tied them, and got up from the bed.

"I'm sorry I snapped. I didn't mean to, and I shouldn't have. But I need you to understand that you can't keep me here. I've been a hunter for a long time, and I have no intention of stopping. I realize I'm only human, but that doesn't mean I don't have the power to keep people safe, and if there's anything I can do, I'll do it. I wouldn't put myself or the others in danger by going out there if I was still in pain or if I felt I wouldn't be able to fight."

Gary looked at his feet. What could he say? Nothing he could think of would stop Chris from leaving. Chris had already made his decision, and it wasn't to stay with Gary while the others headed out on the hunt.

"Gary?" Chris asked.

When he reached for Gary, Gary quickly stepped back. "You should go. I'm sure that whatever's happening is important."

Chris stayed still for a moment. Gary didn't look at him, but he watched him from the corner of his eye as he grabbed a few more things around the room and left. He only relaxed when he heard the sound of the front door opening and closing, but his relief didn't last.

What had he done? What if something happened to Chris, and the last thing they'd said to each other was that? What if Chris was distracted because of what Gary had said and got hurt again?

Gary dropped onto the bed and buried his face into his hands. He could run after Chris, but what would it accomplish? It was better for him to leave Chris alone so that he could focus on what he was about to do.

Fight Kudlaks.

Chris was frustrated. He tried not to think about it as he made his way to Clay and Rowan's house, but he couldn't avoid it.

He understood where Gary was coming from. After losing his entire family and his clan in that attack, he was terrified to lose his mate, too. The fact that Chris had been recently wounded didn't help. That day, Gary had been terrified. He'd probably imagined how close he'd come to losing Chris, and he'd panicked. Since then, he'd been overbearing and a mother hen, and while Chris had tried talking to him about it a few times, Gary had always waved him off. He didn't want to talk about it. Chris had let him be for a while, but when he came back today, they needed to have a serious talk.

Chris couldn't stop being a hunter. When he thought about doing that, his first reaction was that he didn't know what else he could do with his life. More than that, he didn't want to do anything else until he was forced to. He was still young and strong, and he could make a difference. He could save people. Too many had been hurt, including Ronnie, and Chris would do whatever he could to get rid of as many Kudlaks as possible.

But he wasn't sure his mate could understand that, and even if he did understand it, Chris wasn't sure he'd agreed. Gary had allowed his fear to take over, which was why he'd panicked just now when Chris had told him he was going. Of course he didn't want Chris to go on the hunt. The last time he'd fought Kudlaks, he'd been hurt and could have been killed.

But he *hadn't* been killed, and he was back to his normal self. He was confident. He hadn't been lying when he'd told Gary that he wouldn't be doing this if he thought he wasn't ready. It would put him and his friends in danger, and that wasn't something he was willing to let happen.

"Fuck," he muttered as he reached Clay and Rowan's house.

The meeting was brief, and Chris spent the time wondering what Gary would do while he was away. He was relieved when they were finally shimmered to the area where they'd find the Kudlak attackers. From what Clay had explained, they'd hunted a Vila family who'd managed to escape and had sent word to the council. Apparently they'd been headed toward Whitedell to ask about the clan. They were with the council, so they were safe, but Rowan and Clay would go and talk to them once this was over.

Chris cracked his knuckles. It would be over quickly.

He was careful as he and the others entered the decaying warehouse, but as soon as he got his hands on the first Kudlak, he took all his anger and frustration out on him. He was careful not to get stabbed again, but he didn't need to be. With only two Kudlaks this time around, it was easy for a group of hunters to dispatch them.

He punched the Kudlak in the face again, and when the man stumbled back, Chris jumped on him. It brought both of them to the ground, and as he straddled the man's waist to punch him again, he let go of all of his anger. The man's face was a mask of blood, but for some reason, he was still grinning like a monster.

"Your village will pay for this," he said before another of Chris's punches reached him.

"What does that mean?" Kendrick asked.

The Kudlak cackled. "You'll lose everyone you've ever loved."

Chris rolled his eyes. He'd been hunting Kudlaks for years, so he was used to them trying to talk their way out of being killed, threatening them, and everything in between. It sounded like the Kudlak was trying to scare them, which was kind of working. The guy was creepy as he continued to laugh.

Chris punched him again to shut him up. The Kudlak spat out teeth, and it gave Chris a perverse pleasure to know he wouldn't be biting anyone else with those fangs.

"Stop playing with him and kill him," Alexis snapped.

It made Chris realize what he was doing. He'd been hunting for years, but he'd never taken pleasure in hurting

Kudlaks, even after seeing what some of them had done. He'd always told himself that he was nothing like them. He wasn't cruel, and he didn't take pleasure in pain.

But right now, he was taking immense pleasure in hurting the Kudlak. He was taking his frustration out on him, but it wasn't fair.

Chris scrambled back. Alexis arched a brow at him, and Chris shook his head, not knowing what to tell him. Thankfully, Kendrick didn't give the Kudlak the time to get back to his feet. He stabbed him with one of his knives, aiming straight for the heart. The Kudlak's laughter cut off abruptly, and the silence was so loud that it echoed in the cavernous room.

Alexis offered Chris his hand, and Chris took it gratefully, even though his knuckles hurt. He allowed his friend to pull him to his feet, trying to avoid looking at anyone else in the room.

"You're in a mood today," Alexis said.

Chris sighed. "It's Gary."

Alexis grimaced. "He didn't take it well when you headed out?"

"He tried to convince me to stay back. He keeps saying that I'm wounded, even though Nysys healed me. I don't know why, but he got it in his head that the wound is still open deep inside or something like that."

"It would be easier to keep you home if you're still in pain."

"I know." Chris understood why Gary was frightened and why he wanted Chris not to go on hunts, but that was never going to happen. This was Chris's calling, and while he didn't want to give up on his mate, he also couldn't give up on this.

Alexis sighed. "You're going to have to talk to him. He lost everyone he's ever loved, and he's been on the run since then. It's been decades, Chris. Decades of running from Kudlaks, of hiding in the shadows and thinking about the people he lost.

I'm sure you understand why this is hard for him."

"Of course I understand why it's hard. I'm just not sure how to deal with it. I can't give up hunting, and clearly, he doesn't like that. What if he can't accept it?"

"You're going to have to make a choice."

"Is anyone else worried about what the Kudlak said?" Kendrick asked as he pulled a cell phone from the pocket of the Kudlak's jeans.

"About the village?" Chris asked.

"Yeah. How did he know we came from the village?"

Chris and Alexis looked at each other. "The news that there's a new clan has been going around," Alexis said. "It's why the Vila family was coming to us. They found out about the village and want to be a part of it."

Chris grimaced. "And if *they* know about the village, it makes sense that the Kudlaks would, too. This isn't good."

Alexis's expression was grim. "I agree. I'm just not sure what we can do about it. I'm not surprised the news of the clan is making the rounds, and I hope it'll bring us more clan members, but at the same time, it does make us vulnerable."

"As long as the Kudlaks don't know where the village is, we're safe, right?" Kendrick asked.

"Yes, and there are the wards to consider. Even if the Kudlaks find out where we are, they'll protect the village."

Chris nodded, but he couldn't stop thinking about what Gary had told him. The wards weren't as strong as they should be. There weren't enough Vila in the village yet, so they couldn't make them stronger. There was no way for the Kudlaks to know that, but maybe they didn't have to know it. It would be enough for them to attack and see what happened.

"We should join the others," Alexis said as he clapped Chris's shoulder.

It wasn't painful anymore, but Chris still winced.

He looked down at the body on the ground. The Kudlak was dead, so he wouldn't be answering any more questions. Hopefully, the other Kudlak had said more, but Chris wouldn't be surprised if she hadn't. This one had been slightly unhinged and had probably just been trying to scare them. Even if the Kudlaks had plans to attack the village, they couldn't do it because they didn't know where it was.

Right?

Waiting at home on the couch wasn't helping Gary. He didn't think anything would help as he waited for Chris and the others to return, and while he was tempted to go to Clay and Rowan's house to wait like some people did, this time, he couldn't. He remembered too keenly the last time this had happened. He'd been there when Chris had returned with a knife sticking out of his back, and Gary couldn't stop himself from thinking about it every time he walked past the house. He was sure that if he went there now that would be all he'd be able to think of, and that wasn't what he wanted.

He also couldn't stay at home. He'd tried everything to distract himself, from making himself a cup of tea to working in the yard. He'd cleaned up the guest room Chris had used, knowing his mate would probably return to his own home after today.

Gary had no idea where they stood. He hadn't begged Chris to stop being a hunter, but he'd come close, and Chris had to know it. He had to have seen how angry Gary was, how terrified he felt, yet he'd still gone on the hunt.

Gary sighed and got to his feet. Obsessing over this wouldn't help. He'd been wrong, and he knew it. The only thing he could do was apologize to Chris when he returned and hope his mate would give him another chance.

He quickly undressed, knowing the perfect thing to distract himself. It had been a while since he shifted, mostly because while he'd been on the run, there hadn't been a safe place for him to do it. Shifting made him feel vulnerable. He had to get naked to do so, and when he shifted back, he was once again naked. It would be easy for a Kudlak to attack him then, but at the village, he didn't have to worry about that. He could free the beast inside of him out to run.

Vila could turn into pretty much any animal they wanted, but they tended to have favorites. Gary did, and he couldn't wait.

He left his clothes on the couch and opened the back door. His yard gave onto the wooded area that surrounded the village, so he'd get from one to the other without problems.

He sucked in a breath, and for a moment, he enjoyed the warmth of the sun on his skin. Then, he shifted.

He stomped his front feet on the ground one by one, then shook out his mane. The horse wanted to run, and since that was why Gary had shifted, he let go of his control. Here, he didn't need to worry about how people would see him. He just needed to be himself, free and happy, even if it was only for a moment.

He ran through his backyard and into the forest. He moved around the trees, kicking his feet and making as much noise as he wanted. A human scream would worry people if they heard it, but not this.

What would Gary do if he could never get over his fear that something would happen to Chris while he was on a hunt? He couldn't forbid Chris to be a hunter, and he didn't want to. It wouldn't be fair to either of them, and it would make Chris unhappy. Gary couldn't ask his mate to choose between him and being a hunter, but that meant he'd have to accept what Chris was. He'd have to accept the fact that Chris could get hurt and probably *would* get hurt.

This time, Chris had been lucky. Even though he'd been stabbed, the wound hadn't been too deep, and Nysys had quickly healed it. What would happen if the wound was worse the next time? What would happen if a Nix couldn't get to Chris in time? Gary would lose him, too, and his heart wouldn't be able to survive that.

But could he really worry about something that might or might not happen and allow it to ruin his relationship with his mate? He was sabotaging their relationship and his own happiness, and he didn't want that to continue. He'd spent decades mourning the people he loved and running for his life. He wanted to be happy now.

But for that to happen, he would have to allow it.

He didn't know how long he ran, but he didn't want to leave the wards, so eventually he headed back toward the village. He took a different route, which was the only reason he saw the car parked on the edge of the road that led into the village. The car was just outside the wards, so Gary was wary of it, but when he reached it, he found a single man sitting inside, both of his hands grasping the steering wheel as he stared ahead.

Gary frowned. Who was the man? Since he was here, he might be a Krsnik or maybe a hunter. Gary was sure he wasn't a Vila because he didn't look like one.

He hesitated. He'd be naked if he shifted, but if he wanted answers, he didn't have a choice.

He walked closer to the car in his horse form. The man noticed him, and his eyes widened. For a moment, they stared at each other. Gary stayed still, not wanting to scare the man, and he was satisfied when the man opened his door and slid out.

"Okay, I'm not sure what I'm doing, but there are two possibilities here," the man said. "Either you're an animal, and you don't understand anything I'm saying, or you're a shifter."

Gary quickly shifted and grinned at the man. "The second

86

one." Kind of, but this was a quick explanation that fit and that a human would understand.

The man looked away, probably to avoid staring at Gary's naked body. "Okay. Good. I suspected you were a shifter, but you can't be sure these days."

"It's fine. Can I ask what you're doing here?"

The man rubbed the back of his neck. "My name is Ronnie. I was told I'd be welcome if I moved here, and I decided to take that step." He gestured at his car, and now that he had a better look, Gary could see it was full of boxes and bags.

He didn't have to ask to know who Ronnie was. He'd heard the name often. "You're Chris's best friend."

Ronnie's eyes lit up. "You know Chris?"

Gary nodded. He didn't know if Chris had told Ronnie that they were mates, and considering the tense way they'd left each other earlier, he didn't think that spilling the beans would be a good idea now. If Chris wanted to tell his best friend about Gary, he could do so himself later.

"I do know him. He'll be happy to see you."

"Yeah, I'm sure he will be. He's been talking my ear off about the village since he moved here, and he made it sound like the most perfect place on earth."

"I wouldn't say it's perfect, but it's a great place to call home." Gary offered Ronnie his hand. "I'm Gary."

Ronnie shook it before quickly releasing it. "That's good to hear. And I'm really welcome, then?"

"Of course. Why don't you follow me into the village? I'll take you to Chris's home."

Ronnie relaxed. "That would be great."

Gary knew a bit about Ronnie's past, so he could understand why the man was so nervous and kept glancing around. The sooner he got to Chris's house, the safer Ronnie would feel.

"You don't have to worry about the wards. You're not a

Kudlak, so they'll let you in," he quickly explained before shifting.

Ronnie seemed pleased at the news of the wards. He quickly got back into his car and followed Gary into the village and toward Chris's house. Everyone they passed turned to stare at Ronnie, but he didn't seem to care. His focus was on the road in front of him.

Gary shifted back once they reached Chris's house. "This is where Chris lives. He's out right now, but he should be back soon. You know him better than I do, but I'm sure he won't mind if you go inside."

"Thank you for your help," Ronnie said.

Gary smiled at him. "You're welcome."

Gary didn't know how this would change the relationship between him and Chris, but he'd find out soon enough.

Chris was tired but pleased with how the raid had gone. There had only been three Kudlaks, but one of them had managed to escape, so Chris and the others had gone after him. They'd managed to catch him, and they'd killed him while he cursed at them that they would all die.

Weirdly, he'd been the only one to die.

A few hunters had been wounded, but everyone was all right, including Chris. Now that he didn't have to worry about the hunt, he was starting to worry about Gary and how they'd left things.

What would he find when he got home? Would Gary refuse to talk to him?

"You don't look happy," Kendrick said as they gathered to shimmer back to the village.

"It's Gary. He tried to convince me to stay home instead of coming today."

Kendrick grimaced. "He doesn't want you to be a hunter."

"I understand his point of view, but I can't give this up."

"I get it. I mean, I can see both points of view. He lost everyone he'd ever loved to the Kudlaks, and now he's scared to lose you, too. I don't blame him, especially after you were wounded."

Chris huffed. "I'm perfectly fine. Nysys made it sound worse than it was, but he apologized after healing me, so it's fine. I don't need you or anyone else to worry about me."

"Maybe not, but we're still going to worry. So will Gary. No matter how many promises you make him, you can't promise you'll come back every time. We've lost many hunters over the years, and I know you're aware of how lucky we were. We're still here, but not everyone is."

He was right, but Chris couldn't see himself leaving the hunters. He still had work to do, and he was young enough to hunt Kudlaks for a few more years. The problem was that he might have to choose between his work and his mate, and he didn't know what to do.

Kendrick knocked their shoulders together. "Talk to him."

"As if it's that easy."

"I never said it was easy. I'm sure it's not, but I wouldn't know since I haven't met my mate. I just mean that you're not going to find a solution if you don't talk to him."

Kendrick was right, but Chris couldn't go to Gary's house in the state he was in. He wanted to shower the Kudlak blood off his body, and he needed to be a bit more relaxed before he and Gary talked things out. He didn't know what kind of mood Gary would be in when Chris got to him, and he wanted to be ready to face him.

After they were shimmered back to the village, they quickly scattered. Chris headed to his house, ignoring the few people trying to stop him. They weren't who he wanted to talk to right now.

He was almost at his house when he noticed the car parked

in front of it. He blinked and cocked his head, knowing he'd seen it before but unable to place it for the first few seconds. Even after he recognized it, his brain couldn't make sense of what he was seeing. There was no way Ronnie was here, right?

Chris quickly climbed the porch steps and threw open the door. He never locked it. No one locked their door in the village. They trusted each other.

Chris could hear voices in the kitchen, so he rushed in that direction, bursting into the room in time to see Ronnie smile at Gary. They were sitting at the kitchen table, both of them sipping on something warm in mugs—tea, if Chris knew them.

The two parts of his life had just collided, and Chris could only stare.

Both Ronnie and Gary had looked up when they heard him come in, and they quickly got to their feet. Ronnie beamed at Chris, who could only smile back and open his arms. When Ronnie threw himself into them, it was as if something clicked.

Chris's life was once again complete.

"I'm going to go," Gary whispered.

Chris couldn't allow that to happen. "Wait." He stepped away from Ronnie but kept a hand on his arm as he reached for Gary. "What happened? How are you here, Ronnie?"

"I decided to take up your offer and move to the village," Ronnie explained. "I wasn't sure where to go, but Gary found me."

"You two need to talk," Gary said.

Chris turned to him. "We need to talk, too."

"It can wait."

Chris wasn't surprised Gary was trying to avoid the conversation they needed to have. He was tempted to do the same and stay here to celebrate Ronnie's decision to move, but he had a choice to make.

In this situation, it was fairly easy.

He looked at Ronnie. "I'm going to go with Gary and spend the night at his house. Will you be okay here on your own?"

Ronnie blinked while Gary's face turned bright red.

"Why would you spend the night at his house?" Ronnie's eyes widened. "Wait. Is he your mate?"

"Yeah. He didn't tell you?"

The two of them turned to Gary, who looked like he was contemplating running out of the room. Chris dropped his hand from Ronnie's arm and grabbed his mate's waist, pulling him closer. Gary's face went even redder, which was adorable.

"No, he didn't tell me," Ronnie said slowly. "And when you told me you'd met your mate, I don't think you told me his name."

"I apologize," Gary said. "I didn't know if Chris had told you about me, and I didn't want to say something I shouldn't."

"I was an asshole earlier, so I want to go with Gary and apologize," Chris explained. "We also need to talk. I can stay if you're not okay being here on your own, but you're safe and protected."

To Chris's relief, Ronnie nodded. "Gary told me about the wards. I think I'll be fine, but tomorrow, I want to spend time with you."

Chris dragged him closer and kissed his forehead. "I promise we will."

Since Gary still felt tense as a rod, Chris didn't waste time. He dragged him toward the door, waving at Ronnie before leaving the house.

"You really should stay with him," Gary offered.

"Now that he's here, I can spend as much time with him as I want later."

"You can do the same with me. I'm not going anywhere."

"Damn right, you're not. After what happened earlier, we need to talk."

Gary sighed.

Chris had taken his hand so he wouldn't risk Gary running from him, but he didn't think Gary would. He seemed resigned.

"I shouldn't have left you when we were both angry, and I'm sorry I did," Chris said. "I understand why you're so anxious when I go on hunts, but I still have a few good years in me to be a hunter. I'd like to think that what I do makes a difference, especially with what's coming. We both know the Kudlaks are planning something, and I don't want to give up being a hunter before it happens. I have a feeling we'll all need to be ready for what's coming."

"You're right, and I understand how selfish it is for me to ask you to stop being a hunter. I never meant to, and I still don't. It's just hard for me to accept that my mate puts his life in danger every day by fighting the people who killed my family."

"I'm sorry you lost everyone you loved, and I can't promise I'll never be hurt or that I'll return after every fight, but I'll do my best. I'm not giving up on life, Gary. I have you and Ronnie, Kendrick and Boyd, and everyone else. I care about you, and I intend to live a very long life." He hesitated. "Would it make you feel better if we bonded?"

The relief was evident in Gary's expression, but he quickly hid it, as if he was afraid Chris would notice. "I can't ask you to do that just to make me feel better," he said.

"You're not asking me. I'm offering."

Gary frowned. "You realize that if we bond, that's it. You can't decide to leave me."

Chris hated that his recent behavior had made Gary think he might decide to leave him. He'd been hesitant about their bond, but not because he didn't want Gary. "Our life is fucked up, and unless all Kudlaks die or come to their right mind, it's going to be that way for a while. That's the main reason I was so hesitant. I was afraid to tie myself to you because there's a chance I might not return when I go on one of the hunts. I can see that trying to keep distance between us isn't going to work, though. Maybe bonding will make you feel better about me going on hunts."

"At the very least, I could feel that you're all right," Gary murmured.

They'd reached his house and were standing in the front yard. Chris could see people in the house next to Gary's, but his entire focus was on his mate. "If it makes you feel better and helps you accept that I'll continue being a hunter for the foreseeable future, I want us to do this."

"As long as you're sure you won't regret it."

"I'm pretty sure that's one thing I can promise I won't feel." Chris wasn't making that promise lightly. Things might be complicated, but with Gary in his life, he had the best reason to return every time he went on a hunt. He wanted his mate to be hopeful about their future and to know that he was all right even when he was outside the wards.

Chris pulled Gary into his arms. "Let's do it, then."

Gary reached back to open his door. Chris pushed him inside, then slammed the door shut with a foot.

Since he'd been staying here, he knew where Gary's bedroom was. He grabbed his mate's ass and urged Gary to jump, which he did with a sweet giggle that made Chris smile. Gary wrapped his legs around Chris's waist and allowed him to carry him deeper into the house.

Chris might not know what tomorrow would bring for either of them, but as long as Gary was in his life, it would be fine. He was sure of that.

When they reached the bedroom, he tried to drop Gary

onto the bed, but Gary wouldn't let go of him. As a result, they tumbled down together, making Chris think of the first time they'd kissed. They'd been in a similar situation, but it had ended very differently.

"You're going to have to let me go if you want to get naked," he murmured as he kissed down Gary's jaw.

"What if I don't want to?"

"Get naked?"

"Let you go."

Chris tightened his arms around Gary and kissed him. "Even if you do let me go, I'll come back to you."

Gary hesitated for a moment before loosening his hold on Chris. Chris loved that he trusted him to return, and he was aware that their words had more meaning than what was happening right now. If it was in Chris's power, he would always return to his mate.

He hadn't had time to shower, but Gary didn't seem to mind. As soon as they were both naked, he opened his arms to Chris, and Chris couldn't resist. He should probably head to the bathroom, but maybe they could do that together later.

Gary wrapped his arms around Chris instantly when he landed on top of Gary again.

It was as if Gary was afraid to let Chris go, which Chris could understand. He knew that whatever would happen between them next, it would have to happen without them separating. Gary felt too vulnerable to let go.

With Gary, it didn't matter if the sex was quick or slow. There were feelings in every movement they made, and Chris made sure Gary could feel them. Even with Gary not letting go, Chris touched every inch of Gary's body he could. He ran his fingertips up and down Gary's thighs, then around him, gently cupping his ass and spreading his cheeks. Gary wasn't willing to let go for this, either, but he was thrusting with his hips, and both their cocks were hard.

Chris wiggled a hand between them and brought their cocks together. Gary sucked in a breath, and when Chris looked at him, he noticed the glinting of fangs where there hadn't been any before. Gary wasn't a shifter. He'd told Chris that he could choose what animal he wanted to shift into, unlike shifters, who could only shift into one animal. As far as Chris was concerned, that was incredible, but then, everything about Gary was.

Including the fangs that were about to sink into Chris's neck.

"How do I drink your blood?" he asked as he pressed closer and tilted his head to the side.

Gary blinked for a second as if he didn't understand the question, then raised a hand. He moved in a flash, but Chris saw the claw on his finger. It was only there for a moment, but it was long enough to open a long scratch on Gary's neck.

Chris didn't have any instinct when it came to bonding because he was human, but he knew what to do. Squeezing his hold on their cocks, he leaned forward and licked a long stripe along the cut. Gary's blood was coppery and warm, and while it wasn't Chris's preferred drink, he still sealed his lips over the cut and sucked hard enough to get more.

He jerked when he felt Gary's fangs sink into him. His hold on their cocks loosened, but the bite wasn't that painful, and as soon as Gary started drinking, it was easy to ignore the sting.

It was even easier when Chris started feeling his mate at the back of his mind.

It was odd. Chris knew those feelings weren't his, but at the same time, he was feeling them. He could sense how happy Gary was, how much he yearned for him, and how horny he was.

That made two of them.

Chris moved his hand faster. Gary keened, but the sound

was muffled against Chris's neck. He dug his heels against the top of Chris's ass cheeks as if he wanted them to be even closer. That wasn't possible, unfortunately.

They were as close as two beings could ever be.

With the bond between them snapping into place, Chris could feel how relieved his mate was that this was over. From now on, he'd be able to feel if Chris was in trouble. Chris had no doubt that even though Gary didn't have a clue how to fight, he'd find a way to him. He'd save him if he ever needed to be saved.

And even better, he'd love him for the rest of what Chris hoped would be a very long life.

He panted against Gary's neck, moaning as he came. The cut on Gary's neck was a little swollen, but it wouldn't stay there for long. It would heal, but unlike the bite on Chris's neck, it wouldn't leave a trace. Chris felt a bit sorry about that, but it didn't really matter. Gary was his, and no one could separate them.

Gary shuddered in Chris's arms, coming right along with him. They were messy and sweaty, and they'd have to change the sheets, as well as shower if they didn't want to be stuck together for the rest of the night, but Chris couldn't remember the last time he'd felt so at peace. He didn't want the moment to end, so even though he rolled to the side, he took Gary along with him, pulling him against his body and wrapping his arms around him.

"Thank you," Gary whispered.

Chris kissed the top of his head. "There's nothing to thank me for. I wanted this as much as you did."

Chris could feel Gary wasn't convinced, so he pushed the happiness he felt through the bond. He felt like an idiot and had no idea if it worked, but when Gary relaxed against him, he knew it had been the right thing to do.

Chris doubted Gary would ever be comfortable with him

being a hunter, but he knew his mate wouldn't demand he stop. Gary understood how important this was, both to Chris and the people he protected. The upcoming weeks and months wouldn't be easy, but Chris was ready to compromise to make Gary happy.

And he could feel that Gary was willing to do the same.

CHAPTER SIX

Things were going relatively well. Gary was still a ball of fear most of the time, but he'd come to accept that no matter how terrified he was, Chris wouldn't stop being a hunter. It was good that the two of them had talked things out, but the fear was something Gary had to deal with on his own.

If only he knew how to do it.

He looked sideways at where Chris was stretched out on the grass, his eyes closed, only wearing his jeans. He looked incredibly handsome in the sunlight. To be honest, Chris always looked incredibly handsome. Gary wanted nothing more than to stretch out next to him, but he was harvesting mint, and he needed to focus on that.

Just knowing that Chris was there, safe and sound, was enough for Gary to allow himself to look the other way. He continued his work, but all of his fears flooded back in when he heard Chris's phone rattle in the grass next to him. He stopped moving and held his breath to listen to what Chris would say about whatever was happening. It could be a text from Kendrick or Alexis, but somehow, Gary doubted it. Things were getting worse, and the hunters had been going out on hunts more and more often. They were taking turns, so Chris had stayed home recently, but Gary had always known it wouldn't last forever.

"Dammit," Chris swore. "I have to go."

Gary swallowed and told himself not to freak out. It was the last thing Chris needed. He had to be able to focus on his safety and the safety of the people he'd be hunting with, and

98

he wouldn't be able to do that if he was wondering what Gary was doing and if he was freaking out.

Gary put down his basket and knife and turned to his mate. Like this, half naked in the sunlight, Chris looked indestructible. He was made of flesh and bone, though, and Gary knew how fragile that was.

He still forced a smile on his lips. "Will you let me know when you return?"

Chris frowned and cocked his head. "Why wouldn't I?"

"I don't know. We have no idea what's going to happen or how long you'll be gone."

"I'll let you know," Chris promised. "I don't want you to worry about anything."

Gary wanted to tell him that just wasn't possible, but he didn't dare. "I know. I'll do my best."

Chris smiled. "I suppose that's as good as I'll get." He finished dressing, then strode to Gary and cupped the back of his neck with one hand. "I promise I'll be fine. I always am."

Gary couldn't stop thinking that Chris would always be fine until the day he wouldn't be, but he couldn't allow that thought to show in his expression. Instead, he leaned forward to kiss Chris. "Be careful and return to me," he murmured.

"I will. It's a promise."

Gary wanted to tell him not to make promises he wasn't sure he'd be able to keep, but instead, he pressed his lips together. He wanted to go with Chris to Clay and Rowan's house and wait there until Chris returned, but it might be hours. Besides, he didn't want Chris to realize just how nervous he was. He could probably tell, but Gary didn't want him to be worried.

"You'll tell Ronnie what's going on?" Chris asked as he stepped back. "I'll text him, but this'll be the first time I have to go on a hunt since he moved here, and I know he'll be worried. Maybe the two of you can spend some time together."

Gary liked Ronnie, but he couldn't think of anything worse than the two of them waiting together. He felt like they'd push each other to new levels of anxiousness, which wasn't something anyone wanted.

He had no doubt that having Ronnie move here from the city had been a good idea, but at the same time, it had made Ronnie more aware of what Chris's work with the hunters meant. When he'd been away from Chris, he'd only had a vague idea. He'd known it was dangerous, but now that he was in the middle of things, he was bound to see people getting hurt, including Chris. He might freak out, and Gary wasn't sure he could deal with that.

He was freaking out enough on his own.

Chris started to move away but stopped. Gary wasn't sure what was going on until Chris returned quickly toward him, grabbed his waist, and pulled him into his arms. The kiss they shared was a promise that Gary would make sure Chris kept. No matter what happened, Gary would have Chris back. He was ready to go look for him if it was necessary.

He really hoped he wouldn't have to because he never wanted to see a Kudlak in his life ever again.

Chris eventually had to let go of Gary, but Gary tried clinging to him. When they finally separated, he swayed a little. For some reason, the sight made Chris smile.

"I'll see you soon," he promised.

Gary could only nod. This time, when Chris walked away, he didn't return to Gary. He walked around the house, and Gary was left alone.

He sucked in a breath. He wouldn't be alone forever. He wouldn't even be alone for long. Chris would be back in a few hours, and they could continue living their lives.

Gary had to believe that.

Gary finished what he was doing with the mint and brought everything inside. He walked around his house, putting things back in their place and cleaning a bit, but when he looked at the time, only twenty minutes had passed. It would be a while before Chris would return.

Gary couldn't stay in the house. He felt jittery, and while he didn't want to go for a run in case Chris came back early, he also didn't want to feel like a beast in a cage. Maybe taking a walk would help. At the very least, it wouldn't do anything bad, so Gary decided to go for it.

He quickly washed up and left the house. The summer day was gorgeous, and he couldn't help but think about the contrast of the weather and what Chris and the other hunters were doing. It felt impossible that such a bad thing could happen during a day like this, but Gary's clan had been destroyed on a gorgeous spring evening, so he knew better. Kudlaks didn't care about the weather. They didn't feel the cold like humans might, and while they tended to attack at night, they didn't worry about whether it was raining or snowing. They just wanted blood.

Gary shuddered and walked faster. He saw several people gathered in small groups, probably waiting for the hunters to return, but he didn't join them. He continued walking until he reached Chris's house, and when he saw Ronnie sitting on the porch, he hesitated. He wouldn't mind spending time with Ronnie and getting to know him, but he didn't want the two of them to make each other even more anxious than they already were.

Ronnie looked up and saw Gary, which Gary guessed meant that he wouldn't get a choice. He waved, and Ronnie waved back as Gary quickly walked toward him.

"I saw everyone gathering at Clay's house. Chris texted me, so I know they left, but I don't have any details. Do you know what's happening?" Ronnie asked.

"I don't know anything more than you. Chris doesn't tell me much because he knows it freaks me out, but considering what's happening, we can guess they went to take care of a nest."

Ronnie shuddered. "I was only attacked by one Kudlak, and I can't imagine having to face an entire nest of them."

"They don't usually work in groups. They do when they attack a big group of people, but most of the time, the hunters only face one Kudlak."

"But you wouldn't be surprised if this was a nest?"

"The Kudlaks have been behaving strangely, and that's part of it." A part they didn't understand, but then Gary didn't think he could ever understand Kudlaks.

"Chris will be fine. He's been doing this for years, and while he's gotten hurt before, it's never been anything permanent. I know you're worried, but he can take care of himself."

"I know." But knowing that wouldn't stop Gary from worrying. Until Chris was back home with him, his every thought would be on his mate.

The place looked like every other place Chris and the hunters had raided. Kudlaks hunted humans, so they hid in small towns or cities, where they tended to hide in abandoned buildings. Apparently they didn't care about comfort and didn't need water or electricity. They only cared about blood and easily hiding to kill the humans they captured.

Chris was sure not every Kudlak was like that. He just had to look at Melissa, the Kudlak who lived in their village. She'd been hiding in a similar place when they'd found her—an abandoned house that had been crumbling onto itself—but only because it had been necessary. She hadn't been there to hide bodies or have a discreet place to kill people. She'd been protecting her daughter and Devon. She hadn't had a family beyond them and no one to help her, yet she hadn't killed humans. She'd done what she could to raise her daughter right, something Chris admired.

He didn't know what to think of Melissa, but he could admit she didn't seem like a bad person. She hadn't given them any kind of trouble now that she lived in the village. In fact, every time Chris saw her and her family, they all seemed happy and relaxed.

But Chris wasn't happy and relaxed right now. He eyed the abandoned warehouse in front of them. It was quiet, so much so that it was hard to believe there was a nest of Kudlaks in there.

"You know what to do," Rowan said in a whisper.

They did. He'd already briefed them on what he knew about the place. He'd gotten word a small nest of three or four Kudlaks was hiding here. It was a massive building for so few people, which meant it was going to be a bitch to search.

Chris shivered. It wasn't the first time he'd had to deal with something like this, but he didn't like it.

He never did.

He stuck close to Kendrick and Alexis as they entered the building. Boyd had stayed home this time, but Chris wouldn't be surprised to see him popping up like he had the time Chris was wounded. He still came on hunts sometimes, especially when someone had been hurt, but he was also pulling away, which was good because it was what he wanted. It was odd not to fight next to him, but Alexis had taken his place, and he was just as good—probably better, considering he was a Krsnik and had been born to kill Kudlaks.

They were silent as their group separated when they entered the building. Kendrick, Alexis, and Chris went down one hallway, all of them ready to jump into action if they found the nest. Chris could hear himself breathe, the sound of their footsteps, and the few noises the others made in different parts of the building, but that was it.

He frowned as he looked around. There were only a few

entrances in the building, and the one they'd taken hadn't looked like it'd been used recently, especially not by Kudlaks. Usually, the hunters found traces of blood at the very least, but there was nothing like that here. There was plenty of humidity and mold, along with mouse droppings, dust, and plants that had started to grow in the cracks in the pavement, but no blood and no stench of decomposition.

Had they found the only neat Kudlaks in the area?

"I don't like this," Alexis muttered.

Chris was glad to have confirmation from someone who knew more about this than he ever could. "It doesn't feel like it usually does," he agreed.

"Most of them are messy fuckers, but there's no mess here."

"They're probably deeper in the building."

Alexis's expression was grim as he nodded. They continued walking down hallways, clearing rooms as they went. It wasn't cold, but Chris still felt shivery. He expected something to jump out of one of the rooms as they checked them, but nothing ever did. It was as if the building was empty.

He swallowed. Why would it be? Maybe the information Rowan had gotten was wrong. Maybe the Kudlaks had already left. If that was the case, though, they would have left bodies behind.

But there was nothing.

They finished checking the area they'd been assigned and found nothing. They retreated back to the entrance from which they'd come, all three of them eager to find out that everyone else was all right. Several people were already there when they got to the door, and their expressions mirrored what Chris was feeling.

Something was wrong.

Rowan and Clay eventually arrived. "Anything?" Rowan asked.

Most people shook their heads, but Rachel and Caroline exchanged glances, and Rachel nodded. "We did. There was a nest here, but they're gone. I don't know when they abandoned the place, but they left you a message."

Rowan set his jaw. "Show me."

Chris was still careful as they all followed Rachel down the hallway. They might have cleared the place, but he wouldn't put it past the Kudlaks to hide somewhere and jump out at any moment. They were vicious and cruel, but they were also smart.

Terrifyingly so.

No one and nothing jumped them, though, and they reached a room that appeared to have been a breakroom of some sort. Chris had no idea what happened in this warehouse when it was in use, but there were no traces left of whatever work had been done there. He didn't really care, anyway. The place had been abandoned, and it would be better to raze it to the ground than allow Kudlaks to use it.

The breakroom did look like a place where a nest had lived. It was strange how the rest of the warehouse was neat, but this room wasn't. There were traces of blood on the ground, and the air smelled of decay. Chris was pretty sure he noticed a severed hand in a corner, but that wasn't what got his attention.

No, that was the message on the wall.

Clay snorted. "Dramatic, aren't they? Is that written in blood?"

Rowan's attention was on the wall. "It is, from the smell." He stepped closer, and so did Chris. He was curious to see what had been written, but his gaze went straight to the body by the wall. From the looks of it, the man hadn't been dead long, and the blood on the wall came from him. His open eyes stared at the ceiling, and his too-pale skin made it obvious that there wasn't a drop of blood left in his body. Whatever the Kudlaks hadn't used to write on the wall, they'd drunk.

Chris swallowed as he turned his attention back to the wall. There was nothing they could do for that man.

Your village is next.

That was it, but there was no doubt the message was meant for Rowan. He was the one who had started a new clan with his mate and had put together the village.

Chris's stomach churned. He and Alexis looked at each other, and Chris knew they weren't the only ones to think this was bad.

"It's a trap," Kendrick said.

Clay swore, and almost as one, everyone started running toward the entrance. Not everyone had come with them to check the message, and the two Nix who'd shimmered them here today had stayed behind. They were enforcers, and while they were trained to fight, fighting Kudlaks wasn't what they did. They were here for support and to shimmer them if anything happened.

Something had happened.

There was no way to know what the intention behind the words on the wall was exactly, but the threat against the village was clear. It might just be a coincidence, but Chris wouldn't be surprised if they shimmered home to find that the village was under attack. Even if it wasn't, he needed to get to Ronnie and Gary. He had to make sure they were all right and that nothing had happened to them. He could feel Gary through their bond, but the bond felt sluggish, and he wasn't sure why.

They all barged into the entrance, making the two Nix and the few other people hanging around with them jump. Thankfully, the Nix were trained, so they could tell right away something had happened. By the time Chris and the others reached them, they'd already extended their arms, offering their hands to shimmer out.

Chris touched the nearest Nix and got ready for whatever

would greet them when they shimmered home.

A loud screeching made Ronnie and Gary jump. Ronnie looked around, confused, but Gary knew what was happening. His heart raced as he wondered where the attack would be coming from.

The village wasn't large, and most of the houses were clustered around a main road. It cut through the village, and if Gary had to guess, the attack was coming from one of its ends. That would be the easiest way to get into the village.

"What's that? What's going on?" Ronnie asked as he wrapped his arms around himself.

Knowing what he did about Ronnie's past, Gary wasn't sure he wanted to answer. Unfortunately, he didn't have a choice. Ronnie needed to know what was going on. He'd have to hide until this was over.

"We're under attack," Gary explained.

Ronnie's eyes went wide and he seemed frozen, which wouldn't do. Gary knew how he felt. The sound of the alarm was the same one that had echoed around his village so many years ago. It had told everyone they were under attack, but it hadn't saved his clan. They'd all died anyway.

Was his new clan about to die, too?

It was hard not to let the memories pull him in, but Gary fought it. He wasn't on his own. He needed to keep Ronnie safe, and it was clear that Ronnie wouldn't be able to do much on his own. He wasn't even moving to hide.

"I thought this place was safe," Ronnie said in a trembling voice. "I thought I wouldn't be attacked here."

Gary grabbed Ronnie's shoulders and gave him a shake. He didn't want to hurt Chris's best friend, but he wouldn't be able to help if Ronnie was freaking out.

Ronnie's gaze snapped to Gary's. Gary sucked in a breath,

relieved to see that Ronnie was present and not lost in his fear. "I know you're scared. I am, too, and I already went through this once. I know what can happen if we don't react, and I'm not ready to allow that."

"We're all going to die," Ronnie said with a moan.

They probably would, but this time, Gary wouldn't allow the Kudlaks to do what they wanted. If they were going to kill him, they'd do it while he was defending his home and the people he loved.

"I won't let you die," he told Ronnie. "I'll protect you with my life if I have to."

There were tears in Ronnie's eyes, but Gary didn't have time to deal with them. He had Ronnie's attention, and he needed to take advantage of that.

He had so many people he wanted to help. The hunters were gone, but Dermot, Devon, Melissa, and her daughter — all those people were here. They were in danger, and even though Gary knew he wouldn't be able to save all of them, he'd do his best.

He pushed Ronnie toward the front door of Chris's house. "Go inside. Hide."

Ronnie's eyes were wide. "What about you? Where are you going?"

"To help the others."

A different kind of alarm went up, and Gary gritted his teeth. The Kudlaks had burst through the wards. They were coming, and there was no time to waste.

He pushed Ronnie again, not caring how gentle he was anymore. "Chris showed you the hidey-hole he made under the living room floor, right?" he asked.

Ronnie nodded. "He told me it was just in case."

"Well, *just in case* just happened, and you need to use it. Hide under there, don't use any kind of light, and stay as quiet as possible. I promise I'll come back for you."

"You're going to get yourself killed. You should hide with me."

Gary wanted to. He was terrified, and his mind kept going back to the people he'd lost the last time this had happened. He'd felt guilty for their deaths ever since, but now, he had a chance to avenge them and protect the people who were part of his new family. The fear was there, and it probably would never leave him, but he was strong, and he knew he could help.

"I can't," he told Ronnie. "I need to help the others. Please hide and stay safe. Chris would never forgive himself if something happened to you."

Ronnie looked like he wanted to argue, but there was no time. He knew what to do. Gary couldn't force him to hide, but he couldn't waste any more time standing there with him.

He turned and ran, ignoring Ronnie's calls to him. He prayed Ronnie would listen and hide and that when Chris came back, he wouldn't find his best friend dead. It would break his heart if anything happened to Ronnie.

Gary was sure that Chris could feel his panic through the bond by now. He could feel Chris's presence, steady and strong, but not just that. There had been confusion coming through for a while, then a sharp peak of fear. Chris was probably fighting for his life, and Gary did his best to muffle the bond. He wanted to know what was happening with Chris, but he couldn't allow the attack on the village to distract his mate. No matter how terrified he was or how much he wanted to call someone who would take care of the Kudlaks and keep him and the others safe, there was no one to call.

Except that wasn't true.

He swore and took out his phone. Everyone in the village had been given a phone number to call if something like this happened. He was sure someone had already called, but just in case, he did the same as he ran toward one of the entrances of the village.

"We already know," a woman said when she answered. "People are coming to help. The best thing you can do is hide."

A loud scream made Gary jump. He turned to see a Kudlak dragging Melissa out of her house. Her daughter was running after them, crying, while Devon was fighting another Kudlak and losing. He was doing his best, but he was only human.

"Did you hear me?" the woman on the phone asked. "You need to hide. People are coming, and they'll keep everyone safe."

But Gary couldn't hide. He couldn't allow these Kudlaks to hurt Melissa and her family. Devon was already bleeding from a cut on his cheek. The Kudlak holding him cackled and licked the blood that dripped from it and stained his skin. Devon shouted and tried to get free, but the Kudlak was too strong. Gary watched as she grabbed Devon's hair and pulled it to the side, exposing his neck. Her eyes glinted, probably at the thought of the meal she was about to have.

Gary threw his phone at her face.

It hit her right on the forehead, making her jerk away. That was enough for Devon to wiggle his way out of her hold, but like the idiotic, incredibly sweet young man he was, he didn't run, or at least, he didn't run to safety. Instead, he rushed over to Melissa, who was fighting off the Kudlak who'd dragged her out of the house. Her daughter was cowering with her back pressed against the porch steps, hiding her face in her arms.

The Kudlak who'd been about to bite Devon was quick to grab him again. Gary needed to do more if he wanted to save his family.

Even though every instinct he had was screaming at him to hide, he did the opposite. He reached deep inside of himself and shifted.

His favorite animal to shift into had always been his horse. When he was in that form, he felt free and could run. As much as he loved the horse, though, it wouldn't help him here. He needed something stronger, something with claws and fangs.

He turned into a bear.

Bears were fast and massive, and Gary wasn't any different in this form. He stood on his back legs and roared, getting the attention of both the Kudlaks, Melissa, and Devon.

He didn't give the Kudlaks the opportunity to run. He rushed forward, watching with glee as their eyes widened, and they both scrambled away. The woman had let go of Devon, who turned and kicked her in the knee. She yelled and fell on her face, and Gary was on her in seconds.

He'd never killed anyone before, but he didn't hesitate. He slashed at the woman's throat with his claws, feeling them sink into her flesh as if it were butter. Blood spurted, and her eyes widened. She tried to get away, but Gary sank the claws of his other hand into her heart.

He didn't pause to watch the light leave her eyes. He turned toward the other Kudlak, who was running.

Gary ran after him.

As they shimmered back to the village, Chris couldn't stop thinking about what was happening there. They were under attack. Rowan had told them he'd gotten a text from several of the people who lived in the village to warn him that the alarm was ringing. This had been a trap, and the Kudlaks had used the opportunity of having the hunters at the warehouse to attack the village.

Chris would tear them to pieces with his hands if they hurt anyone he cared about.

He couldn't imagine what Ronnie and Gary were going through. Ronnie had come to the village after Chris had promised it was safe, and now, here he was, under attack by Kudlaks like the one who had ruined his life.

And Gary. He'd gone through this once before. He'd lost his entire clan and family and every person he'd ever cared about. This had to bring him back right to that moment, and Chris hated the panic and fear he could feel through their bond. He could tell that Gary was trying to shield him from it, but the emotions were too strong.

When they finally reached the outskirts of the village, no one waited for Clay or Rowan to give orders. Thankfully, the leaders didn't seem to care. They didn't try to stop anyone. They just raised their weapons and ran forward.

There didn't seem to be that many Kudlaks, but the wards weren't strong, and it looked like the Kudlaks had managed to breach them because there were so few of them. Not that it mattered. Chris was going to kill every single Kudlak still standing.

He wanted to run straight home, but he couldn't avoid stopping when people needed him. Two Kudlaks were attacking Dermot and Tamlin. He was surprised to see those two in the thick of things, considering what they'd gone through before, but they were fighting the Kudlaks with kitchen knives and pans. As he watched, Dermot slammed the cast-iron pan he was holding into the face of a Kudlak, breaking the woman's nose, if the loud crunch was an indication of anything. She screamed, but not for long. Chris came up behind her and slashed her throat, and Tamlin stabbed his kitchen knife into her heart.

The two appeared bewildered, but Chris didn't have time to take care of them. As much as he wanted to make sure they were all right, his fear and panic pushed him to go home. He needed to find Ronnie and Gary. He needed to make sure they were okay.

He couldn't read the feelings coming through the bond.

Gary was scared, which was to be expected, but he also felt smug. That didn't make sense, which was why Chris was sure something was wrong.

He ran down the road, only to come to a stop at the sight of a massive brown bear running after a man. From the blood on the man's clothes, he was ready to bet he was a Kudlak. He'd never seen a Kudlak run away from anyone, though. Even when the hunters attacked, they fought back.

Not this one. He was screaming and running for his life, but he wasn't fast enough. The bear caught up to him, jumping onto the Kudlak's back and slamming him into the ground. The Kudlak's scream abruptly cut off, and Chris watched as the bear tore out the Kudlak's throat.

Blood spurted all over the dry earth. The bear was still for a moment before climbing off the Kudlak's body and looking around.

Maybe he was looking for more Kudlaks to kill.

There were none. Chris could hear the sounds of the fighting vanishing now that the alarm was gone. They were replaced by a heavy silence that made him want to sob. The village shouldn't be silent. It should be full of people talking and laughing and living their lives without fear.

The Kudlaks had ruined that. They'd barged into the village, attacked the people who lived there, and scared and possibly killed them.

"Chris!" Ronnie's voice yelled.

Chris blinked at the sight of Ronnie sitting on the ground by the house, holding Melissa's daughter against his chest. The only thing Chris could see of Haley was her blonde hair, but as much as he liked the little girl, she wasn't who he was focused on.

Ronnie's eyes were wide, and tears tracked down his cheeks. Why was he here? Didn't he realize that the girl he was holding was a Kudlak? She would never hurt him, but

Ronnie couldn't know that, and considering his past and the fear he had of Kudlaks, Chris didn't understand what was happening.

The bear turned, and his gaze stopped on Chris, who was standing there like an idiot. For some reason, he readied himself to fight even though he knew this couldn't be a normal bear. There were no bears in the area—not of the real bear variety, anyway.

He wasn't surprised when the bear started shrinking, but he *was* surprised to realize that the bear was his mate.

He ran forward, not one moment of hesitation now that he knew who the bear was. When he reached his mate, Gary was completely naked. His skin was bloody, and Chris's fear spiked.

"Are you hurt?"

Gary's face was covered in blood, but that probably was because he'd bitten a Kudlak or two. The sight was grisly, but it reminded Chris that his mate was alive.

Gary shook his head. "It's not my blood," he murmured.

Chris ran his hands over Gary's arms, shoulders, and chest. As far as he could see, it really wasn't his blood. There were no wounds on him, not even a scratch.

He pulled Gary into his arms. "What the fuck happened? Why aren't you hiding?"

Gary stiffened into Chris's arms and took a step back. "Because I hid the last time this happened, and I lost everyone. I wasn't going to allow it to happen a second time."

Chris sucked in a breath. He understood what Gary was saying, and he wasn't angry or hurt. He would have done the same thing. He couldn't have stayed behind when his village was in danger.

He dragged Gary back into his arms and kissed the top of his head. "I know. I'm proud of you."

Gary shuddered. "I killed two Kudlaks. I'd never killed

anyone before."

"You did what you had to do to protect yourself and your family. It was the right thing to do."

Gary slumped against Chris, and for a moment, they stayed there, holding each other up. Chris could see Ronnie and the others over Gary's shoulder. Ronnie was talking to Melissa and trying to convince Haley to let go of him, but he wasn't having much success. Devon was there, too. There was a long cut down his cheek, but he didn't seem to care. He was focused on Melissa and Haley, although that didn't last long when he turned toward Chris.

"Where's Kendrick?" he asked.

Chris shook his head. "I don't know. When we shimmered back and realized what was happening, I ran for Gary and Ronnie."

Devon frowned. "You're supposed to protect Kendrick."

"I'm sure he's fine."

"You can't know that."

Gary put a hand on Devon's shoulder. "We can't know that he's fine, but listen, Devon. The fight is over."

While Chris could hear people calling out to each other and someone crying nearby, the sounds of swords and knives hitting each other were gone, as were the snarls and taunts from the Kudlaks.

He looked down at the Kudlak Gary had killed in front of him. The man was bleeding out in the dirt, and Chris had to resist the urge to kick the body. The Kudlak was dead. He would never hurt anyone ever again, and it was thanks to Gary.

Chris hugged him tightly. "I could feel how scared you were, but it was as if you tried to cut me off from the bond."

Gary sucked in a breath. "I thought you were fighting your own fight, and I didn't want you to focus on me." He shivered. "I was terrified."

"But even though you were scared, you didn't hide. You stood up for your village and fought. You killed two Kudlaks."

Chris hoped this would help Gary heal the wound he still carried from when his clan had been attacked the last time. He hadn't been able to help anyone then, but he had this time. Chris prayed Gary would never have to go through this again, but if he did, he'd be all right. He finally knew how strong he was and that it didn't matter that he was a Vila and wasn't trained to hunt Kudlaks.

He'd saved his village by being himself.

CHAPTER SEVEN

It had been days since the attack, but Gary was still pissed. He suspected he would be for a long time.

Yes, he'd helped his village. He hadn't cowered like he had the first time around, and he'd killed two Kudlaks.

He still wasn't sure what to think of that or how to deal with it, so he'd decided to shove the feelings he had over the situation to the back of his mind and focus on something that was more important.

Protecting the village.

The wards had failed. There hadn't been that many Kudlaks attacking, yet the wards hadn't been strong enough to keep them back. They'd attacked together, and they'd managed to break through the wards. Thankfully, the alarms had warned Gary and the others of what was happening, but it wasn't enough. They needed to raise stronger wards and keep the Kudlaks out of the village permanently.

Which was why they needed more Vila.

"You know, your phone is already in bad shape after you threw it at that Kudlak's face. I wouldn't be surprised if you managed to set it on fire just by glaring at it."

Gary turned and glared at Chris instead. He was sprawled on the couch in Gary's living room, looking like he belonged there. His bare feet were on the coffee table, and he was wearing shorts and a t-shirt. He was sipping on a bottle of water, not one scratch on him after what had happened the other day.

Gary's heart raced. He wanted to climb into his mate's lap,

but he had work to do first.

"My phone is fine," he said, even though the screen was cracked. He considered it a good sacrifice since it had helped him defeat a Kudlak. When Clay had offered to replace it, Gary had waved him off. He didn't need a new phone, especially not with this one being proof of how strong he was.

It felt odd to think of himself like that, but he *was* strong. He was also much braver than he'd ever thought he could be.

And he wasn't the only one. When he'd left Ronnie at Chris's house, he'd expected the human to hide. He was pretty sure Ronnie had expected himself to do the same, but instead, he'd gone after Gary. He'd told Gary he was afraid of something happening to him and that he didn't want Chris to have to go through that, but Gary wasn't sure that was the truth. Maybe Ronnie had been too scared to stay at the house alone, or maybe he'd panicked and had tried sticking with Gary.

Whatever the case, the result had been that Ronnie had been out during the fight, and he'd seen Gary kill two Kudlaks. When he'd noticed Haley hiding by the porch, he'd pulled her into his arms to protect her. He'd made sure she didn't look at the fight and had shielded her from the blood and death. Gary was relieved she hadn't seen that, and he knew Melissa was, too. She'd been thanking Gary and Ronnie profusely every time she saw them around the village.

By some miracle, they hadn't lost anyone. The hunters had returned from their raid just as the Whitedell pride had burst onto the scene. There hadn't been much for any of them to do. From the last count, only eight Kudlaks had been found dead around the village. Gary had killed two of them, and he'd heard that Dermot, Tamlin, and Chris had killed another two. Gary wasn't sure about the last four, but something told him there had been more than eight. Eight Kudlaks were a lot to fight, but the wards shouldn't have broken down so easily.

The other Kudlaks had probably run when the hunters and the pride had arrived. It was a relief, but it still didn't allow Gary to stop worrying about what would happen the next time they attacked. They knew how weak the wards were now. Even though they also knew that the village was protected, they'd done enough damage as it was. They'd only needed a few minutes in the village to hurt people.

But no one had died. Gary wasn't the only one who'd fought. Even though everyone had been terrified, they'd stood up to the Kudlaks and defended their new home. They'd do so again if necessary, but Gary wanted to make sure they wouldn't have to.

Which meant it was time to call the numbers he'd memorized.

He couldn't be sure these people would still have the same phone number or even if they'd still be alive, but it was worth a try.

"Come here," Chris said as he straightened on the couch.

Gary was too nervous to sit next to him, but like always, he couldn't resist. When his mate wanted something, Gary gave it to him, if it was in his power.

This was.

Gary dropped onto the couch next to Chris. He was still clutching his phone, and while he knew he didn't have to do this now, he wanted to. He was nervous because he didn't want to find out that people who'd been on the run with him and that he'd briefly considered friends were gone or had been hurt, but the village needed them. They might also need the village. If they wanted a place where they could be safe and to stop running, the clan would welcome them. Being nervous wasn't a good enough excuse not to give them this opportunity.

His fingers shook a bit as he dialed the first number on his phone. Chris wrapped an arm around his shoulders but didn't pull him close, allowing him to move as he wanted. No matter how much he wished to snuggle against his mate, he needed to get through this first.

"Yes?" a woman answered, sounding suspicious.

Gary cleared his throat. "Larra?"

"Who's asking?"

"It's Gary."

It took Larra a moment, but eventually, she remembered Gary. "Of course. I didn't expect to ever hear from you when I gave you my phone number. You didn't have a phone back then."

"I wouldn't have one now if it weren't for my new clan."

Larra was silent for a moment. "You're part of that new clan everyone's been talking about?"

"Yes."

"Sounds nice. Why are you calling me?"

"I'm going to be honest. The clan is still small, and we have a village to protect. I don't know if you're still on the move or if you found a place to call home, but if you haven't, you're welcome to come here."

"You need more of us to protect the village."

"We do." Gary might as well be honest. He doubted Larra would want to come if he lied to her. He didn't have a reason to. Even if she said no, she could still pass on the message that the clan was looking for more people.

"Tell me about the clan."

Larra's request wasn't a surprise. After all, if she was going to move here and settle down here, she'd want to know what to expect.

Gary stayed honest as he explained about the village, the Whitedell pride, and clan members. Vila were used to living with Krsniks, but that wouldn't be the case here, at least not entirely. There were many more human hunters than Krsniks in the clan at the moment, and it would take some time getting used to. Gary didn't have a problem with it, but other people might, including Larra.

She listened to everything Gary had to say without interrupting him. He didn't hide the fact that the village had been recently attacked because there was no reason for him to. Larra could find out if she knew who to ask, and Gary had no doubt she did. She'd probably look into the village and every single member of the clan before making her decision.

Gary couldn't blame her for that. He'd do the same if he were in her place. When he, Dermot, and the others had found out about the clan, they'd looked into it before deciding to try to reach them. They hadn't known if it would be a good fit for them, but they'd been willing to try because what else could they do? They couldn't stay out there, being hunted by Krsniks for the rest of their lives.

The same went for Larra and every other Vila who was still on the run. They all deserved to be safe and not have to run ever again, and that was what the village offered.

Hopefully, she and everyone else they contacted would take that chance. The village needed them and had a lot to offer.

ABOUT THE AUTHOR

Catherine is the creator of several series, most of them paranormal, including the Whitedell Pride Series and the Gillham Pack Series. While she graduated in translation, she decided to go the writer's way because it was more fun to create her own stories and characters.

She's been living in Italy for more than twenty years, but she's a daughter of the North—Belgium to be precise—and she misses it so much that she's already planning to move back.

She loves pizza—probably too much—her son, her pets, and of course, books. She sneaks some reading time into her schedule every time she has five minutes free from writing, demands from her various pets and son, and lastly, housework.

Connect with her:

lievens.catherine@gmail.com
BookBub: https://www.bookbub.com/authors/catherine-lievens
Website: https://authorcatherinelievens.com/
Facebook: https://www.facebook.com/catherine.lievens.9
Facebook Group: https://www.facebook.com/groups/411788002341528/
Twitter: https://twitter.com/authorCLievens
Newsletter: http://eepurl.com/c-uvKn

www.ingramcontent.com/pod-product-compliance
Lightning Source LLC
Chambersburg PA
CBHW060635130626
46555CB00002B/806